MW01115503

With Spring Comes Love

Ruby Jackson

With Spring Comes Love

Copyright 2015

Author is owner of this book. All rights reserved. No portion of this book may be reproduced by any means without the written permission of the author except for short excerpts for publicity articles or reviews.

Other Books by Ruby Jackson

In a Series:

Quest for Love

Love's Mountains to Climb

Seasons to Grow

Love Conquers All

Single Books:

Secret in the Cellar

Brotherly Love

Bible scriptures quoted from the King James Version.

The book cover is a photo of the log cabin my great grandparents built circa 1890s. It is called a dogtrot or dog-run cabin due to the opening between the two sides. One side was used for housing while the other was for the storage of food supplies and other items. The people in the photo are ancestors on my father's side of the family.

This book is a work of fiction. Any resemblance to real people is a coincidence. Author does not know of any person or persons living or dead who lived similar lives.

About the Author

Ruby Jackson began her writing career in 2009 after retiring from twenty-five years of teaching. She lives in Arkansas and enjoys being near her children, grandchildren, and great-grandchildren.

Ms. Jackson has enjoyed writing since she was a young girl. Growing up in Texas, she moved with her family to many different towns throughout the state. Some years she went to two or three different schools in one school year. Books became her best friend as she grew up and she read avidly wherever the family moved. Her imagination has led her to write poetry as a hobby to writing Christian romance fiction now that she has time to enjoy the stories she wants to put on paper.

As an adult Ms. Jackson has belonged to the same church for many years. She has taught Sunday school and Missionettes and is currently the Women's ministry leader.

One of Ms. Jackson's loves is to travel across the United States and she hopes to be able to visit every state while she can. She enjoys learning the history of each state she visits and imagines what it would have been like for the people in the early years of statehood.

Most of Ms. Jackson's books are set in the 1800s but she does write in other time periods such as the early 1900s. Books already written have been set in the Panhandle of Texas, Napa Valley of California, Boston, Massachusetts, and in the Ozarks of Arkansas at the time of this writing.

She credits her love of writing to her mother and to the many teachers who helped bring her imagination to life. They helped her to open her mind to history and gave her a love of the great nation she was born in. She prays teachers continue to inspire and excite students to want to explore our history and visit the places that have made America what it is today.

Introduction

A dark time in American history took place between 1860 and 1865. Lives were changed forever. A new America came out of the Civil War that had pitted the Northern States against the Southern States.

Thousands of America's sons were killed on the battlefields scattered throughout the states. Brother fought against brother. Uncles, cousins, and friends chose the side their conscious took them and fought until there was no life left in them.

There were also those who fought more as renegades than soldiers. They were paid mercenaries who raided towns and communities, killing whosoever got in their way. They burned fields and stole what supplies and money the people had.

Many weary Union and Confederate soldiers became prisoners of war and lived in camps not fit for humans. Lives were snuffed out in those camps as were those on the battlefields. Those who survived carried scars physically and mentally.

As the war came to a close, many of those in prison camps were freed only to find their homes gone and families scattered. Their lives were shattered. Only a small fragment of hope existed in their lives. They grasped at straws to give them the hope that would carry them forward into the unknown. They needed to believe there was a new beginning for them somehow, somewhere.

With Spring Comes Love

Ruby Jackson

"Boys, get the rest of that corn into the crib. We don't want to leave it in the field where the deer will eat it," Caroline Hollister chided as she picked up corn stalks and stacked them. "Make sure the animals can't get into it. It will have to last all winter."

The two red-haired boys finished throwing the dried corn on the cob into the sheet and pulled the ends together. Each took two ends as they carried it to the corn crib and dumped it on top of other cobs that were already there.

"Maw, can we go down to the crick now?" one of the boys yelled.

Caroline looked up and frowned at the boys. The frown didn't last long. Before her stood identical twins from the top of their red heads to their booted feet.

My sons, the pride and joy of my life, she chuckled, *spoiled, conniving, little boys with hearts of gold.*

With a sigh, she turned back to the cornfield. There were more stalks to be stacked and then they needed to be taken to the shed.

Work and more work, she thought, *it never ends.*

This wasn't what she had expected when Thomas moved her to the Ozark Mountains of northern Arkansas. Mountains covered with trees and vines and nothing else except rocks on top of rocks. Mountains with little tree filled ravines and valleys where small creeks dried up or slowly trickled down in late summer and rushed out of their banks in the spring after heavy rains.

Mountains and valleys where there were no towns and only a settlement that took a day to get to. Mountains with neighbors miles away in little valleys and hollows like the one she was standing in.

Looking toward the cabin, she wiped her face and shook her head. The house was a cabin with a dog-run through the center. The logs were rough hewn and dark from the weathering. The chimney, with its curling smoke floating skyward, was made partly of rocks, mud, and sticks.

No, it wasn't what she had expected at all. She had left a large whitewashed house with cotton fields stretching in every direction. A house where there were bright curtains and a parlor to invite guests into. There was a cook and housekeeper that took care of all the household chores. Meals were a time to reflect on the things she and her brothers had done during the day. A time to visit with her father and watch as he became animated over things he had seen in Little Rock.

The man, who worked outside, kept the yard filled with flowers and shrubs. It was always admired by the neighbors for being a showcase of beauty. Caroline loved to have parties in that yard where her friends could drink tea and eat scrumptious desserts made by the cook.

There were also two men who worked in the fields. Her father had an overseer who made sure the fields were properly taken care of. He worked along side the two Negroes, who lived on the plantation, to plant and harvest the cotton in the fall.

One more worker took care of the stable and the fine horses that were kept there. How she longed to take the long rides with her friends through the fields and into the trees where the bayou ran.

"I miss Bayou Bartholomew," she muttered as she picked up more stalks. "I want to wade in the water and teach my boys how to catch crawdads and let them get a cane pole and line and catch catfish. I really miss the cypress trees, the riverboat's whistle, and the flat land where I could see forever. I want to ride my horse into the wide open fields with the wind blowing through my hair like I used to do and eat picnics along the bayou with my friends and family. Oh, how I miss the parties and fine clothes that I wore when out on the lawn with my friends. I so miss my friends. Especially Mary, she was the best friend a girl could have."

Sighing, Caroline wiped strands of hair from her face. A tear sparkled.

"Most of all I miss Mama and Papa. I want to see them so bad. Letters aren't enough. I want to see for myself that they are well. And, I want to see my brothers and their families. I want to see how the children are growing. My boys need to know their cousins!"

She threw corn stalks against others she had already stacked. They slightly slid down the side.

"And, I miss Livvy's mayhew jelly and hot biscuits. Oh, how I miss Livvy and all the talks we had in the kitchen while I munched on those biscuits!"

Shaking her head, Caroline picked up several more stalks and laid them together.

"Maw, who are you talking to?" Timmy asked, pulling on her sleeve.

"What? Oh, no one, I was just talking to myself. Have you finished the corn?"

"Yes, Maw, we have. Can we go down to the crick now?"

"I will give you one hour and then you have to get back to work," she gently answered. "And, I mean it, boys, you will have to get back to work. There are still lots of work to do."

"Yes, ma'am!" the slightly shorter of the two boys yelled over his shoulder. "Come on, Tommy!"

"Tommy, remember one hour! Timmy, remind him!" she yelled back.

"All right, Maw!" the other boy answered, moving ahead of Timmy. "I'll remember!"

"Yes, Maw!" Timmy yelled back.

"I can't believe I am letting them get out of work again," she muttered, picking up more stalks. "Their father would never have put up with this behavior."

With all the cornstalks stacked, Caroline sat down on a large rock and stared after the boys. They were wading in the cold water. Looking back at the valley, Caroline sighed and lowered her eyes to her hands. They were red, scraped, and raw. Her fingernails were jagged and broken into quicks.

No, this wasn't what she had expected. She knew a house would have to be built but she thought it would be large with possibly white columns and large windows looking out at distant mountains. She didn't expect one large room where one end was used as a kitchen and the other as a living area. Behind the kitchen was the bedroom. It was so small only a bed, her chest, and one chair would fit. A tiny window looked out toward the shed. Across the dog-run was where the

canned and stored food was tucked away each year.
Cured hams hung from the ceiling and bacon covered
with salt was put away in a barrel.

Shaking her head, Caroline turned back toward
the boys. They had been so small when they had traveled
to the mountains. She had torn them away from their
grandparents, uncles and aunts, and cousins that they had
grown to love. They had traveled for weeks going into
the unknown and not knowing anyone who would be
living in the mountains close to the Missouri border.

Caroline let her mind drift back to the green
delta five years prior to the present. She pictured the day
they left the comforts of the big roomy home on the
plantation she loved. A part of her wanted to stay but the
love she had for her husband drove her to comply with
his wishes.

Chapter 2

As her little family left the farmlands of the Delta, she had been weary of leaving her home. Her life was being left behind. She watched as miles of cotton fields, wheat fields, and small towns gave way to larger towns and the flowing Arkansas River. She had been to Little Rock but no further north. Her father had only taken her to the river's edge and let her watch the ferry as it slowly made its way across the water.

After a time, Caroline watched the lowlands as they gave way to winding roads leading through valleys and up over dark blue mountains. The going was rough. As the wagon climbed to the ridge of a mountain more mountains could be seen in the distance. It looked endless. Days of tiring wagon travel came on the heels of quiet evenings around a campfire and peaceful, protected sleep under the stars beside the man she loved.

The fire cast long shadows along the ground as they prepared for a night of rest. Thomas filled the night with his guitar as the boys laughed and clapped their hands. The shadows danced with them as the flames burst up in red, orange, and yellow flickers. The birds awakened them at daybreak and there would be another day of mountains and valleys after a breakfast of cold meat or boiled eggs.

When she thought she couldn't take another day of riding in the jostling wagon, they turned and followed a stream through a valley. Cliffs and forest were on both sides of the valley. A couple of days later the wagon came to a small creek that was trickling out of the forest. Thomas turned into the woods on a trail so narrow that the wagon barely fit. After what seemed like half an hour the forest opened into a small valley. An old log house stood close to the trees, the back of it embraced by the shadows.

Thomas became animated as the cabin came into view. His excitement couldn't be contained. As soon as the wagon stopped, he was jumping from the seat and yelling to the occupants of the house.

Caroline had been more constrained. She had never met Thomas's family in the six years they had been married. She was nervous. She didn't know what to expect.

The door had opened and a bearded man and a younger man stepped out. Turning, the older man called back into the house and soon a gray-haired woman emerged. Thomas and the woman embraced and shouts of joy rang out in the valley. The young man grabbed him next and dancing a jig they jumped around the yard.

Last, the man grasped Thomas by the shoulders and pulled him close.

Running back to the wagon, Thomas had pulled the boys from the wagon then took the small bundle Caroline was holding. Holding one of her hands, he helped her down and returned the bundle to her.

"Mama," he had said, "this is my wife Caroline and our two boys and daughter."

Turning to Caroline, his face had shined. "Honey, this is my mama, and papa, and that over there is Joseph. He's my little brother."

Caroline nodded at the trio and tried to smile. It was nervous and didn't come off the way she wanted it to.

But it didn't matter. Caroline was embraced by the woman as the boys were scooped up by the man. Quickly, the woman began to uncover the precious little girl that was in the bundle. The child stretched and frowned. Both women laughed and the older woman motioned for everyone to enter the house. Caroline felt more at ease.

It had taken a month for the men to fell trees and make a clearing at the edge of the rows of trees and undergrowth. The trees were rough hewn and laid aside until enough were cut. A few days later two more men arrived and work began on the home Thomas and Caroline would call theirs.

But, for Thomas it was short-lived. A month after the house was finished he was gone; gone back to the Delta. Back to Caroline's brothers and the war that was dividing the nation.

Caroline sighed again and shook her head. It happened so far back that it seemed like a dream.

"Five years," she whispered. "Five years we have been here. Five years of terror. Five years of hard work during the summer and five years of cold lonely winters. Five years without Thomas."

Straightening, she looked toward the boys. They were still wading in the water. She watched as they stood still and then quickly reached down into the water with both hands. Smiling, she shook her head.

Trying to catch fish, she thought.

After watching them for a few more minutes, she changed her position. Her eyes moved from them and scanned the valley. Everything was quiet. The only movement was the boys. Even the dogs were lazing in the sun.

Standing up, she stretched and headed toward the edge of the woods. The shed, used to house the cow, came into sight as she rounded the end of the cabin. It was almost invisible in the shadows of the trees. Almost, but not quite. Leaves that once adorned the tall trees were gone. Bare limbs protruded from the heavy trunks. Sunlight filtered through and beams of light highlighted the ground.

Pulling her long-sleeved shirt closer, Caroline shuddered. Cold air lingered in the shadows and bit the nose. Looking around, she noticed dark clouds were making their way over the mountain tops. She could hear an occasional distant rumble.

"I need to put the rope up between the cabin and the shed," she said aloud. "Never can tell what the weather will change into."

Quickly, she grabbed the long rope and tied it to the metal ring on the shed. Carefully, she unrolled the rope and carried the other end to the house where she repeated tying the rope to another metal ring.

"Maw, we caught three fish. Can we have them for supper?" Tommy said behind her.

Turning, Caroline held her hand to her chest.

"Tommy, you scared the death out of me! These are trying times. Don't sneak up on me like that!"

"I'm sorry, Maw. I didn't mean to sneak up on you. Can we have the fish for supper?"

Caroline looked at the three fish. They were nice sized and enough for supper.

"We will have to scale and clean them. We don't want to leave any of it near the house when we are finished. I don't want to wake up to bears being around the house!"

"If'n I had a knife of my own I could clean those fish," Tommy said, holding the fish up to look at them again.

"Well, you don't have a knife and you don't need one. I will take care of the work myself. You boys have plenty of time to grow up and learn to do those kinds of things."

The fish were frying when the boys entered the house.

"Maw, Tommy made me carry the bucket up the ridge by myself. He should have helped me!" Timmy, the other twin said as he exploded into the house. "Tell him next time it's his turn!"

Caroline rolled her eyes and ignored the jabber. Quarrels were never ending. If it wasn't over fish entrails it was over checkers or cards or something else.

"Boys, wash up and get ready to eat. It will be getting dark soon. We need to put Brownie in the small shed tonight. She needs to be up where she is easier to milk in the mornings. And, don't forget the calf!"

"Yes, ma'am," Timmy answered. With eyes widening, he smiled. "I put her up last night. It's Tommy's turn to put her up!"

"I need help if it's my turn," Tommy answered. "You know Brownie don't like me."

"Doesn't like you," Caroline answered.

"That's what I said," Tommy replied with a smirk.

"Timmy, just help him. Let's not argue."

Caroline was finished with the dishes and throwing the dishwater out back when the boys came up to the stoop.

"All done," Timmy said.

"Thank you, boys, you are a big help." Caroline answered over her shoulder as they entered the cabin. Picking up her knitting she busied herself with a pair of stockings for herself.

Caroline heard the wind pick up. She could hear it in the attic. The low moan wasn't bad, just enough to whisper and make the house seem haunted.

Grimacing, she looked toward the small, narrow window facing out from the front of the house. She hated the harshness of late fall in northern Arkansas. The house was sturdy but the wind and cold always seemed to creep into the rooms. As winter approached the boys had to be moved out of the attic and into a corner of the big room. It was too cold for them to stay up there. Joseph and Thom had kept the house chinked but it just didn't seem to be enough.

If Thomas had stayed longer the house would have been built sturdier, she thought, *but he didn't stay. He was in a hurry to leave so he could fight in the war.*

With a sigh, she laid the stockings aside. After working in the field all day, she was too tired to work on them.

Turning, she watched the boys on the old rag rug play with the horses her husband had carved.

Her husband, the love of her life; gone forever.

The war had taken everything from her. He had marched onto the battlefield to never return. The letter had said he fell bravely at Gettysburg with his comrades of the Arkansas infantry. Now he remained there forever.

Sighing deeply, she turned back to the window. The rain was getting heavier.

"It's time to go to bed, boys. As soon as you are ready I will tuck you in and help you with your prayers."

Stoking the coals in the stove, she made sure there would be coals left for morning. She cleaned some of the ashes out of the fireplace and added extra wood to the live coals.

"We're ready, Maw," Tommy yelled.

"Honey, you don't have to yell. I am right here," Caroline answered. "I'll be with you in just a minute."

Wiping her hands, Caroline moved to the side of the bed. Smiling, she kissed each one. "Who wants to go first?"

"I do!" Timmy replied, putting his hands under his chin.

As the prayers were finished, Caroline tucked the quilt around them.

"I love you boys," she quietly said. "It's time to go to sleep. I will see you in the morning."

Timmy watched as his mother walked away and picked up the bucket she had put the ashes in. He watched as she carried it out the door and disappeared into the dark. Quietly he turned to his brother and whispered to him. Turning onto their backs, they placed their hands under their chins and prayed once more.

Rain was still falling when Caroline awakened the next morning. She stared at the gray sky and sighed. Pulling on her dress, she headed to the kitchen to make coffee. She hoped the coffee would perk her up.

"Boys, it's still raining. Everything is wet out there. I have to go out to the shed. The cow and calf need to be fed. I need to check the chickens also," she said after breakfast.

"We can do the chores, Maw. It's our job. You just stay in where it's dry," Timmy answered as he jumped from the table.

"Yeah, Grampa says we are big enough to help you all the time and that we should do all the outside work. I agree with him. He's smart. Besides, I need to stretch my legs," Tommy chimed in.

"You are such precious boys," she replied, "Just like your father. He was so eager to please. And yes, Tommy, I know what your grampa said but I'm not sure I'm ready for you to start doing everything."

"Tommy says that just because he likes to be outside," Timmy smirked. "He probably would like to live up in the woods if you would let him! But, then he would have to pull his own weight instead of me doing all the work!"

"Boys, let's not start that again," Caroline warned.

The twins hugged their mother and grabbed coats, scarves, and gloves. Opening the door, they held their heads down as they moved down the run and into the frigid, blowing rain.

Watching from the small kitchen window, Caroline kept her eyes on them as they played around the rope between the cabin and the rough cut wooden building housing the animals. The shed was behind the house and inside the cover of trees. It was almost hidden in the darkness of the shadows.

Slowly the door of the shed opened and the boys disappeared. Smiling, she let a tear touch her cheek.

"Thomas, you would be so proud of our boys," she sniffled out. "If only you were here. Nine year old boys need their father. They need to know the love only a father can give. It's just not the same as mine."

Turning to the pie safe, she prepared bread dough for biscuits and then dough for a crust to go on a cobbler. Getting out a jar of grapes in their juice, she opened it and poured it into a pan. Pulling on the dough she pulled it until it would fit the pan. Finally she added sugar and butter to the top. Stoking the fire in the old wood burning stove, she opened the door of the oven and placed the cobbler inside.

"Boys, you will love this," she whispered. "It will be so special for Sunday dinner tomorrow."

As she pulled the biscuits out of the oven, Caroline suddenly realized time was passing. The rain was still coming down. There seemed to be no let up any time soon. Fog had rolled in and made the day dreary.

The boys were still in the shed. Looking out the window again, she squinted her eyes so she could see through the dense fog. She watched as the shed door came open. Both boys grabbed the rope and moved back toward the warmth of the house. Sighing, Caroline moved away from the window, checked the ham she was frying, and picked up the eggs she was going to cook.

She was always on edge when the boys were outside alone. There could still be bushwackers or jayhawkers roaming through the woods and if they entered their little valley the boys would be in danger.

Caroline shuddered remembering the group of men who came into the valley during the war.

"No, no, no! I am not going to spoil this day with such thoughts! The good Lord is not going to let that happen again. Not ever! The war is over. It's all over," Caroline said, looking out the window once again.

Chapter 3

The musty smell of rich, moist soil filled the air. Leaves crunched and twigs broke under the weight of the three people climbing up the incline toward the ridge above.

The temperature of the air was cooling as a breeze snaked its way through the trees. The ground was littered with fallen leaves and more leaves floated down as they were detached by the wind. Acorns thumped to the ground, waiting for furry animals to hide them away for the winter that was fast approaching.

The threesome, moving up the hill at different rates, explored the trail looking for hidden treasures of fall. The first ran ahead with eyes turned toward the tree covered sky for any movement that indicated life in the treetops. The second looking at odd shaped trees with vines wrapped around the trunks that could be used as walking sticks. The third, the oldest of the three, kept an eye on the two ahead and an eye on the shadows where danger could be lurking.

The climb up the densely forested mountain wasn't for pleasure and the two younger climbers were beginning to tire of the climb. Their young minds wondered and explored nearby interests.

"Boys, don't get too far ahead of me," Caroline called to the two bobbing heads darting one way and then another. "Tommy, you know to stay close. Don't go any farther until I am closer."

Tommy threw dry leaves into the air as he waited on the mountainside. It didn't matter that sticks were intermixed with the leaves. He just grabbed and threw.

Timmy ducked and weaved as the sticks came flying toward him. Finally he stopped and waited on Caroline.

"I quit," he said as she arrived where he was standing. "I can't even get close to him when he's like this. I think he's half wild man!"

Caroline laughed and knelt in front of her serious son. Shaking her head, she gave him a hug and then tied his boot.

"Honey, you have to overlook his behavior. You know how he is. He loves the outdoors just like your grampa. He will grow out of it. Someday, he may act just like you."

"I don't think so, Maw. I think he will always love the woods and want to live in the wilderness where he can fish and hunt for his food. You already know he can't wait until you say he can use a gun. He's going to go crazy! No, he will never be like me. I will be the one who gets educated and becomes a man of means. I'll probably have to support him all his life. I'll be the one who grows the crops and does the harvesting. I'll be the one taking care of the farm while he runs off into the woods."

The vision of her two boys living different lives brought to mind the story of Esau and Jacob. Laughing, she shook her head. She could see how they were similar. But, she could also see how different they were.

"Timmy, you are only nine years old! Don't be so serious! Things might not always be the way they are now. You may decide to live here the rest of your life and become a wild man with your brother. Only time will tell. Both of you will make fine farmers. Wait and see. Tommy will outgrow his exuberant fantasies and settle down. Someday he will be a responsible young man and you will look back and wonder what happened to the brother that was so spontaneous."

Caroline gave Timmy another hug and kissed him on the cheek. "You are so sensitive, my sweet son. That's why I love you so much. And, that's why I know you will be patient with your brother. Now, come on and let's catch up with Tommy before he disappears into the woods where we may never see him again!"

Timmy threw up his hands and followed after his twin. Over his shoulder, he threw back one last comment, "I will never be like my brother! I am too much like you! I also don't know how much patience I can have with him!"

Caroline stopped and looked after the boys.

Yes, Timmy was too much like her: serious; to the point; and always trying to make sense of the possible and impossible. Those were the qualities that were going to make him a good brother and a good provider when he grew up

.

The shadows on the mountain were deep. Birds chirped and flew in different directions. Barking squirrels could be heard in all directions. An occasional glimpse of a hawk could be seen through the treetops as he looked for an evening meal.

A fox watched as the trio noisily made their way farther up toward the small clearing on the ridge. Raccoons, 'possums, and deer wearily kept their eyes on them, ready to race off into a more secure area at any given time. Several turkeys scampered into thick brush and disappeared.

Other eyes were lurking in the dense forest as well. The shadows hid the watchful eyes. They watched every move the woman made. Ears strained and listened for any part of conversation that could be heard.

The owner of the eyes eased his way along the shadows and silently breathed with hopes he would not be seen. Cautiously, he placed his feet where they would not crush any twigs or dry leaves. He hoped the birds and squirrels would not give his presence away. He listened to see if the birds became quiet or if the squirrels scurried away because they sensed he was there. They didn't change their actions.

He watched as the woman approached a rickety wooden fence, turned a piece of wood, and opened the small picket gate.

"Boys, stay near the fence," she warned. "I don't want to have to tell you again. I need to know where you are at all times. We won't stay long so be patient."

"Yes, ma'am," they answered in unison.

Stopping a safe distance from the clearing, the man's eyes scanned the area. It was quiet. The only movement was the trio he had been watching. Moving a little closer, he gazed at the small wooden fence encircling several rocks standing upright

He watched the boys going in and out of the large rocks standing upright and then they stopped at one standing alone. They stood there until their mother joined them. He couldn't understand what was being said. He was too far away. A few minutes later the boys ran outside the fence and were exploring.

"Remember what I told you. Stay close," the woman warned again.

"Okay," one of the boys answered as he looked at vines and small trees.

The man squatted behind a large oak and kept visual contact with the boys and woman. He couldn't risk being discovered. Several times he had to hunker down in the shadows as the boys ran through the trees but, to his relief, they never looked in his direction.

Turning his attention back to the woman, he watched as she placed a small handful of colorful fall flowers in front of the rock. She carefully pushed the stems into the ground so they wouldn't blow away.

"Tommy is throwing rocks at a squirrel!" Timmy yelled, breaking the silence.

"Boys! Can't you ever stop fighting?" Caroline spat out.

She was tired of their behavior. There had been continuous arguing and fussing all day. She had hoped taking a walk would have helped them. It didn't.

"They are getting older, they are getting older, they are getting older," she repeated over and over under her breath. "They are individuals, expressing their own unique personalities. I must be patient!"

Looking around, Caroline could barely see Tommy through the undergrowth.

"Tommy, please, you are trying my patience. Stay where I can see you and you can see me. Please!"

A small snicker, coming from deep in the shadows, died in the forest expanse.

Suddenly, Caroline felt hair standing on her arms. Uneasiness engulfed her. Looking around, she tried to peer into the shadows that were getting longer.

Standing up, she smoothed her skirt and tried to stay calm. She felt eyes watching her but couldn't see anything.

Could there be a cougar or panther watching? Possibly a bear? Were they in danger?

"Boys, it's time for us to get back to the cabin. Don't dally behind me. Let's go, now."

The boys ran to their mother and started the trek back down the small trail toward the waiting cabins.

Lord, protect us, Caroline kept repeating, *don't let any harm come to my children. Keep us safe.*

The man sank deeper into the shadows. He knew his presence had been detected. Quietly, he moved his head so he could see the people hurriedly walking down the mountain toward the safety of the valley below. Carefully, he made his way halfway down the incline and positioned himself behind a large rock out of sight. With his head barely above the rock, he concealed himself and waited to move farther down.

But, he didn't go any farther. Realizing darkness was on the horizon, he knew he had to climb back up and leave before he couldn't see anything in his path and possibly lose his way back to his horse.

Disappointed, he waited until the woman was out of sight. He didn't get to see where she went when she reached the floor below. It was lost in the shadows and trees. He didn't know if she walked straight ahead or turned left or right.

Hitting his leg, he slowly began the climb back toward the ridge. He had a ways to go. He hoped he could make it before the shadows overtook the whole mountain and there would be no visibility left. Dense, low-lying clouds were obscuring the last rays of the sun. He would have no light once the daylight was gone. He couldn't rely on the moon coming through the clouds.

Clouds covered the sky and rushed in darkness. He could barely see his horse as he approached the tree it was tied to. Snow began to fall as he mounted the brown gelding on the ridge. Closing his coat, he gave the horse a light kick, pulled one rein to turn the animal around, and started down the backbone of the ridge. He knew the trail would come out a few miles down below in the river valley. His only concern was if the horse would be able to see the trail and stay on it.

It took longer than the man had planned to reach the floor of the valley. The ride was dark and unyielding. As he walked his horse through the valley, a small break in the clouds emerged. Light trickled from the moon that had been hiding behind the clouds. A short time later, he came upon the small trickle of a creek coming from an extremely narrow brush and tree filled hollow between two mountains. Stopping, he looked at the undergrowth protecting the hollow. A carved mark was on one of the trees standing as a sentinel next to a small path leading into the denseness.

"I know you live in there," the man said under his breath. Closing his tired eyes, he took a deep breath. Swallowing hard, he bit his bottom lip. "I know you are in there."

What now, he asked himself. *What do I do now? Was I wrong to come by here? Was it wrong to watch the woman? Have I gone absolutely crazy?*

Clouds moved over the moon and darkness again encircled the man. Another blast of snow began to fall. Moving his horse along, the man stopped about a mile from the hollow and made camp in the heavily wooded hillside. Quickly, he cleared an area under a large tree and started a fire for the night.

Caroline kept looking back as she and the boys moved quickly toward their cabin. She wouldn't be at ease until they were safely behind closed and locked doors.

Once inside, she didn't immediately light the lantern. She waited and watched the hillside through the window. Darkness completely took over the woods. She couldn't see anything moving.

"Maw, are you going to light the lamp?" Tommy asked, innocently.

Caroline sighed. She knew she couldn't continue to stand by the window. She had to stay calm and not get the boys upset. Turning from the window, she struck a match and pulled the globe from the lamp.

There may not have been anything up there anyway, she thought, *I may have imagined it all. I probably just let my nerves get the better of me. Still....*

CHAPTER 4

Caroline tried to let the feeling of being watched pass from her mind. The last of the canning was finished and all the work in the fields was over. She was pleased with the work she and the boys had done throughout the summer and fall. The corn was in the crib and the stalks were tied together and moved into the woods. A large woolen cover had been thrown over them along with wide boards that would keep them dry.

The potatoes were put away under the house and the canned vegetables were neatly put on shelves. Apples, pumpkins, onions, and dried fruit were in the attic where they would stay dry throughout the winter.

A large fire had been built outside for the two women in the hollow to do large quantities of cooking. A large cast iron pot was hung over the fire and was used for making jelly and canning of the vegetables. Sarah had helped her prepare the fruits and vegetables that had been grown in the hollow. They worked hard putting the produce into the jars for canning. It had taken weeks of work but it was worth it. When the canning was finished, Thom brought the maple sap and sugar cane to be made into syrup and sugar. The two families would have plenty to eat through the months that lay ahead.

Caroline giggle at the memory of how the boys stayed close as the sugary treats were cooked down. Finally, after the syrup and sugar were made, they got to eat the candy that was left in the pot.

"Couldn't have done better myself," Thom Hollister said as he cut into Caroline's thoughts. She collected herself and continued showing him around the storage room. As they walked around the shed and the area where the corn and wheat stalks were stored, small drops of water were beginning to fall from the sky. It was almost unnoticeable. "Yes, sir, mighty fine job. I knew those boys were big enough to help this year. They're going to make fine help."

Caroline smiled at her father-in-law. His shoulders slumped but his spirits were high. He had slowed down and Sarah, her mother-in-law, had asked if she and the boys could do more of the work without letting him know she had asked for help. His health wasn't what it had been. Pneumonia, the year before, had taken a lot out of the old man. He wasn't as spry as he once had been.

"I'm glad we could help. The boys need to get some experience," Caroline answered. "I'm also glad we got it finished before bad weather set in."

"Yep, the good lord was mighty kind to us this year. We had a bounty of vegetables and that hog was mighty meaty that we butchered a couple of months ago. We're all set for winter and just in the knick of time. It looks like we might have a fiercesome winter. It happens ever now and again. When it does, we have to buckle down until good weather comes again," Thom answered, looking toward the sky. "I guess I better head toward home. Sarah don't like for me to be out of her sight for very long. It probably will start raining any time anyhow."

Caroline watched as he walked home and then turned her eyes toward the sky. Clouds were beginning to grow darker and scraped the tops of the mountains. Changing weather was inevitable.

Even though winter was just beginning, it was already showing itself to be an unusually harsh season. There had already been a small ice storm at the end of October and there had been a light dusting of snow the second week of November. She remembered that snow very well. The snow had begun as she and the boys entered the cabin after coming down from the graveyard on the ridge.

Timmy and Tommy were able to play in the snow the next morning; tracking the big, flop-eared dog and rolling in the mixture of mud and snow. But, uneasiness still raised its head and Caroline carefully watched for anything abnormal. She didn't see anything.

Now, as Caroline continued to look at the low hanging clouds, a slow steady rain began to fall. The temperature was in the thirties. She worried that the temperature would continue to drop and the rain would turn into snow or ice. She was glad she had put the rope up between the cabin and shed. At least she and the boys could hold on to it when checking the animals whether it was pouring rain, snowing, or icy.

Caroline busied herself in the kitchen after entering the cabin. Tomorrow would be Sunday, a day of rest. She needed to make a pie and bake bread to take to her in-laws. She and the boys could spend the day with them reading, discussing scriptures, and quietly visiting.

As she worked, she could hear the boys playing a game of cards on the rug in front of the hearth. She didn't have time to play a game with them.

The aroma of bread fresh out of the oven mingled with the smell of frying potatoes as Caroline bustled around the kitchen. The warming beans had been cooked the day before. Cornbread from the day before was wrapped in a towel and now on the table. The boys would soon be rushing to the table ready to devour whatever she put in front of them. Leftovers would be eaten for supper on the Sabbath.

"Maw, can I read from the bible tomorrow when we go to Grampa's?" Timmy asked, shoveling more cornbread and beans into his mouth.

"Do you want to?" Caroline asked, surprised. The boys had never asked to read during their Sunday service at their grandparents' home.

"Yes, I think I would," the boy answered.

"Then I will ask Grampa if that will be all right. I think he will be very proud that you want to read from the bible. What about you, Tommy?"

Tommy placed his chin in his hand and looked at his food. Holding his fork, he picked at the contents of the plate. Finally, he looked up at his mother.

"If'n you don't mind, I think I will leave the readin' to Timmy and Grampa. I'm not much good at readin'."

Caroline half smiled and nodded. She was hoping Tommy would be more willing to take part in the Sunday studies, but she didn't want to push him.

"That will be fine, Tommy. I know you listen to the studies and get a lot out of them. The good lord knows when you will be ready."

"He will probably be thirty before he wants to read," Timmy said.

"Will not!" Tommy exclaimed. "I'll read when I'm ready! I don't have to read just because you want to!"

"Boys, we don't have to make this into a shouting match," Caroline shushed. She wished she had not asked Tommy about reading. She knew his reading wasn't very good. He stumbled over many words. She would have to be more careful about what she said. She didn't want to discourage him.

Sundays were always a joy for Caroline. It was before Thomas left that they had started the tradition that continued year after year even though he wasn't there. She and the boys would spend most of the day with Thom and Sarah. There would be bible reading and prayer time. Then Sarah would tell a story from the bible using different voices and actions. Dinner would be eaten in silence and then Thom would play a few hymns on his fiddle.

Sunday was wonderful, a day filled with quiet and tranquility. It was soothing and peaceful. Caroline listened attentively as Thom read scripture and explained the meaning. He asked questions as to how the scriptures should be applied to their lives.

The stories were lively. The boys' eyes would widen as Sarah told a different one each week. Their interaction was priceless. Sometimes they would ask for a story to be repeated and she would graciously tell them she would tell it on another day.

Caroline enjoyed the afternoons the most. She could close her eyes and enjoy the rhythm of the tunes without the boys interrupting every few minutes. They sat in front of their grampa and watched his fingers move on the end of the fiddle, changing the sound of the strings, while his other hand pulled the bow back and forth across the strings.

"Maw, we're ready. Can we go?" Tommy anxiously asked.

Caroline turned toward the boys and smiled. They were standing by the door with boots and coats on.

"I will be ready in two shakes of the squirrel's tail," she laughed.

Walking to the other cabin in the hollow took only minutes. Caroline put on her shawl and picked up the cherry pie she had made for the occasion.

The boys were exuberant and had already crossed the few hundred yards and were knocking on the door.

Caroline kept looking at the mountainside. She still felt eyes were on her from somewhere on the ridge. She was glad when she was in the safety of the cabin.

"Grampa, I would like to read this morning," Timmy was saying as Caroline entered the door.

"I think that is a wonderful idea," Thom was answering. "I do declare you might be a preacher some day."

Caroline touched the boy's hair as she walked by and sat down at the kitchen table with the others.

Thom opened their study with a prayer and then turned in his bible to the book of Second Corinthians. Timmy watched and turned quickly to the same scriptures.

"All right, Timmy, you can start with chapter nine and verse six and read to verse eight," Thom said with a smile.

Timmy's eyes found the scriptures and slowly he began reading:

> *9:6 – But this I say: He who sows sparingly will also reap sparingly, and he who sows bountifully will also reap bountifully.*
>
> *9:7 – So let each one give as he purposes in his heart, not grudgingly or of necessity; for God loves a cheerful giver.*
>
> *9:8 – And God is able to make all grace abound toward you, that you, always having all sufficiency in all things, may have an abundance for every good work.*

As he finished, he looked at his grandfather.

"So, is that why we plant such a big garden and more in the fields than what we can use our-selves? We are supposed to help others?"

"That's right," Thom answered, "we are supposed to help those who don't have as much as we do. I take vegetables, fruits, wheat, and cotton to our neighbors who either don't grow the same things as us or their crops don't make. It's the Lord's will for us to share our bounty. I also take some to the peddler and trade with him so he can take the produce to the settlement and help those people out."

Timmy nodded.

Caroline was proud of her son. He was growing in his understanding of being a Christian.

"Granny, I'm hungry," Tommy said, breaking the silence that had settled in the room.

"Well, I have fried chicken, potatoes, and okra. After dinner we will have the delicious pie your mother brought over. Now, I just need someone to help me set the plates on the table."

Laughing, Thom and the boys quickly left the table. They watched as their grampa put away his bible and settled in his favorite chair.

Caroline got up and moved into the kitchen to help with the meal.

"My, Caroline, this pie looks delicious! I could almost eat it before we eat the meal," Sarah said as she handed it to her daughter-in-law. Picking up a knife, she passed it on to Caroline and then turned her attention toward the beans. "I know how much the boys like ham in their beans so I added a little extra."

Shaking her head, Caroline chuckled. The boys were spoiled. There was no doubt about it. Their granny made sure she made their eyes shine in every way she could.

"The pie is finished. Would you like for me to cut the cornbread?" she asked, quietly.

Nodding, Sarah moved so Caroline had access to the stove where the bread was perched at the back. It didn't take long for the cornbread to be cut and placed on the table.

"This boiled okra and the boiled potatoes will set this meal off perfectly," Sarah said as she put them on the table with the beans. "Mmmm, boys the food is on the table. Get your hands washed and Grampa can say the blessing and then we can eat."

Noise filled the room as the boys raced to the washpan. Soon they were waiting for their grandfather to sit down and say the prayer.

"Lord, we have lots to be thankful for. You have been so gracious to us. You've taken care of us and watched over us. We want to thank you for that and for the food you have blessed on our table today and everyday. Amen."

It didn't take long for the boys to have their plates in their hands. Caroline took one at a time and filled it.

"Granny, you can't even tell this food was cooked yesterday," Timmy said, stuffing beans and cornbread into his mouth.

"Well, that's because I keep the stove warm and place them on it so they will warm up before we eat," Sarah answered with a laugh. "It's not right to cook on the Sabbath. We shouldn't have to think about cooking when our minds should be on the good lord."

Everyone nodded and continued to eat.

"I'm glad you thought about cooking yesterday," Tommy replied as he handed his plate to his mother. He was ready for a refill.

When the meal was finished, the boys sat on the floor near the hearth. It was time for their granny to tell a story.

"Well, this rain reminds me of Jonah and the Big Fish," she said with a smile.

The boys had heard the story many times and listened intently. Occasionally, they added their own voices to the story from time to time.

"God, let me out of the whale!" Tommy shouted in a low voice.

"I won't disobey you again!" Timmy added.

This thrilled Sarah and she told them when they wanted to act out a story, she would help them with costumes and props.

After story time, the boys turned to watch as an old worn fiddle was carefully taken from its case. They sat and listened to slow and fast hymns their grandfather played as he drew the bow across his prized fiddle.

"You play good, Grampa," Tommy said as Thom finished a tune. "Did Paw play as good as you?"

"He didn't play the fiddle," Thom answered, fingering the instrument. "I tried to teach him, but he liked the banjo and guitar. Now, your Uncle Joseph knew how to play. He could really make that bow sing."

Thom stopped for a moment and sighed. "Yes, your Uncle Joseph was really good. He would have been lots better if he was with us today."

Shaking his head, Thom cleared his throat and slowly looked at the boys. He knew he had to be positive. The boys were looking at him with a frown.

"And…and your Uncle Bob plays the fiddle and the banjo. He is really good, too. He can make his fingers dance on the strings when he plays. Yes sir, what music we could make. All of us playing together and switching up the instruments made for a wonderful day of music on that porch out there!"

"Someday I'm going to learn how to play the fiddle like that," Tommy replied. "I want to learn all the instruments so I can sit on the porch and play with you."

"Well, that's a mighty big order to learn to play all the instruments. Maybe you should stick to one until you learn to play it."

Laughing, he rubbed the boy's head. Putting the fiddle back in its case, he put it in the corner. Some day we will see if you have what it takes to learn to play. It takes a lot of concentration to play. I don't know if you are ready for that."

"He's not, Grampa," Timmy said with a nod, "He's got to slow down before he can concentrate. His mind goes here and here and there and there. He can't stay with one thing for very long."

Caroline shook her finger at Timmy. She knew it was true but she didn't like the tone Timmy used or the use of his finger to point in many directions.

Timmy ducked his head and frowned. He knew he was being shamed and would be in trouble when they got home.

Sarah shook her head and changed the subject away from the quarreling boys.

"Your aunt Margaret can play the mandolin and guitar just as well. Maybe she would like to play for us when she comes for Christmas," she interrupted.

"I remember her playing one time when we were really young," Timmy said as he turned to his grandmother. "We were all sitting out on the porch. Uncle Stephen played the guitar and she played the little guitar. And...and you played your fiddle!"

Thom laughed. "That was the mandolin that she was playin'," He answered. "Yep, she played right along with us. Tell you what, when she was a kid she could outplay her brothers. That made them want to practice more and more."

"I remember something!" Tommy jumped around and hollered. "Paw played with everyone before he left! We were all on the porch. But...but there was someone else that played, too. I can't remember who it was."

Thom looked over at his wife and gave her a wink.

"I'll tell you somethin' else, your granny can play mighty fine music, too. Yep, she can make that banjo sing so perty."

"Oh, you know rheumatism has made it hard for me to play anymore," Sarah spat out. "Besides, I never could keep up with all of you playin'."

"It was Granny!" Timmy shouted. "I remember! We sat next to Maw and listened to the music. Maw was crying."

Everyone looked at Caroline. Thom quickly changed the subject and got the boys talking about music.

"Your paw left the next day," Caroline quietly whispered. No one noticed. Everyone was talking at once.

"Your granny needs to get her instrument out and play sometime," Thom was saying.

"I told you I can't play anymore. My hands don't work like they used to. Now, don't you get somethin' started. I'd hate to show the boys who is in charge around here," she answered with a brow raised.

Caroline turned her head to the side and listened to the banter between her in-laws. They were playful and jovial. She couldn't remember a time when they had a real argument. It was always Sarah chiding Thom in her sweet, little voice that ended any problems.

"I think the boys and I will leave before you two get to arguing about playing music," Caroline laughed. "It has been a wonderful day. God is so good. If you need anything, please let me know. The boys and I are always ready to help."

"Thank you, dear, we know you are. I think we will rest for a while after you are gone. Thom is probably worn out and I know I am a little tired," Sarah said as she gave Caroline a hug. Reaching down, she hugged each of the boys and gave them a kiss on the cheek.

"You boys be good now, you hear?" she said with a smile.

The boys ran to their grampa and wrapped their arms around his neck. He patted their backs and smiled.

"Bye, Grampa and Granny. See you later," they called as they hurried out the door.

Chapter 5

By the next week, winter had arrived. The snowstorm had the markings of a storm. Caroline shuttered. She didn't like the feeling. It was hard to be cooped up in the cabin for days. The boys grew rowdy and unsettled. They fidgeted and argued. The only reprieve came when Thom was able to visit and keep them entertained with stories of his adventures in the mountains. With a storm raging, he wouldn't be coming over for a while.

The dogs had awakened Caroline several times during the week. It unnerved her that they barked for two nights in a row. She carefully looked around during the day but didn't see anything unusual.

Thom had heard the dogs as well. He had checked around both houses and walked up on the hillside. He finally decided the dogs were barking at coyotes on the hillside. He and Caroline could hear them at a great distance near the ridge. They were crossing just as darkness filled the woods.

Everything had quieted down by Friday evening. Caroline didn't think anymore about it.

The boys were finishing up the evening chores while Caroline cooked supper. It had been another work day for her. She had been making woolen socks for the boys. Now, she was ready to relax and read God's word before going to bed.

The door opened and a twin entered.

"Where's Timmy?" Caroline anxiously asked.

"He's coming. The man in the shed is going to help bring in more wood. He said it looks like the snow will get deeper throughout the night," Tommy answered, setting the milk bucket on the table.

"Man? What man?" Caroline raised her voice. It shook as the words came out. There wasn't supposed to be anyone in the shed. Then, she remembered the dogs barking.

"We told him it would be all right to come in the house. He's cold and hungry. He doesn't have on a good coat."

Caroline's brow raised and her eyes widened.

A stranger coming into the house? What were the boys thinking?

"It's all right, Maw. He's a nice man. We've been talking to him."

The door opened and Caroline swung around. Panic filled her. Her eyes darted from one boy to the other. Neither seemed concerned. Suddenly, she came eye to eye with the man. His stare was unnerving. His brown eyes seemed to penetrate into her soul.

Caroline steadied herself. Straightening, she spoke with control.

"Who are you and why were you in my shed?" she coldly asked.

The man held his hat in his hands and moved his fingers around the brim.

Caroline looked at the hat. It was worn, dirty, and had the imprint of an emblem that had once been on it; a Confederate emblem. Looking up, she tried to concentrate on the man's words.

"I was just passing through, Ma'am. I mean no harm. The weather…the weather hit and I couldn't see to go any farther. The shed was a welcome sight. I plan to just spend the night and then move on. I'll go back to the shed now, Ma'am. I don't mean any harm."

Caroline observed the man. He looked tired and malnourished. She wanted to tell him to leave, but the words wouldn't come out. With a sigh, she looked at the boys. Both were staring at her.

I can't let him stay, can I? No, no, I can't let him. That would be wrong. But, what if he knew Thomas? What if…?

The man dipped his head, put his hat on, and turned toward the door.

"Maw," whispered Timmy.

Caroline looked at Timmy and gripped a shush at him. She looked around the room trying to find an answer. Staring at the stooped shoulders that were almost to the door, she made a hasty decision.

I can't let him know we are alone. I can't let him see how scared I am.

"Others will be here shortly but you can eat with us and then I will give you some blankets. The hay, along with the blankets, will keep you fairly warm. Thom will check on you in a while. You can talk to him when he comes in. You can wash up in the pan. Boys, don't say anything. Go and set the table."

The tall, thin man looked at the woman turning her back toward him. She was calm, confident, and secure in an aggressive way. He wasn't sure what to think.

Looking around the room, he noticed the boys also had peace and security in the confines of their home. Still scanning the room, he looked for anything that would indicate there were other children; possibly a girl. There was nothing.

Shaking his head, he looked at the back of the woman again before moving to the pan and washing his hands. Tommy instantly was by his side and handed him a cloth. Timmy was setting the potatoes on the table.

Wearily, the man sat down in the chair Timmy pointed toward and put his hands in his lap.

"I'm much obliged, Ma'am. I am kind of hungry. It's been awhile since I had a really good meal."

Caroline turned and looked at the man.

"Who are you and what is your name?" she inquired, trying to keep her voice normal and calm, "Where are you from?"

"My name is James Cartwright. I live down south near the Mississippi. I had a farm there for awhile."

"What are you doing here?" she asked, holding to the back of a chair.

"I'm on my way to Mountain Home. I thought there might be a position at the academy. I heard about it before the war began. A former student came down to the town I taught in. He talked about it being an excellent school."

Caroline cocked her head and gritted her teeth.

"You must have gotten lost, Mr. Cartwright. Mountain Home is northeast of here. It's not even close. We have neighbors close by, but our closest community is Locust Grove."

"Yes, ma'am, I guess so. It's not easy winding your way through these mountains. But, as soon as morning breaks I will head out again."

"So, you're a teacher?"

James lowered his head and wiped his hands on the napkin. The cloth was rough. Home-spun, he guessed.

"I was, Ma'am, before the war. I taught in Monticello. I had the older boys in class."

Caroline narrowed her eyes and searched the man's face. It was rugged and pale.

The war? Was he in the war? Did he see fighting?

Looking at the hat the man had hung by the door, Caroline stared at the spot where the emblem should have been. She bit the inside of her cheek. It had to be an officer's hat. He could have been a captain or something.

Had he been at Gettysburg? Could he have been like so many others and spent his time defending Arkansas? Or, God forbid, could he be a former bushwacker or Jayhawker or... was he still one and got lost in the storm?

Suddenly, Caroline remembered the uneasy feeling she had a few weeks earlier. Hair raised on her arm.

What if he was watching us from the hillside?

Clearing her throat, she looked around the table. Her hands shook. There was no knife at hand. Nothing she could use to defend herself. The closest neighbor was Thom. He was close but not close enough. Because of the wind he wouldn't here if she yelled for help.

She needed Thomas. He would know what to do.

Lord, what do I need to do? I need wisdom. This man could be a killer. He could have been with….

Slowly Caroline's eyes settled on the hot beans that had been simmering all afternoon. She sidled toward the stove and picked up a dishrag.

Straightening, she said a silent prayer and stood by the stove. She had to have strength for the boys. She couldn't let them see her waiver.

"We pray in this house, Mr. Cartwright. Our lives are centered on the lord and his word. Are you a praying man?"

"I am a praying man, Mrs. Hollister. I've been a praying man most of my life and I do read the good book. It has been a comfort to me many times."

James stopped for a moment and crooked his head. Yes, the bible was a comfort to him, and prayer had kept him from going crazy through the long years of war. Clearing his throat, James looked at the woman staring back at him. Slowly he went on.

"I want to assure you, ma'am, I don't mean you and your children any harm. I'll leave if you want me to.

I don't mean to make you nervous but I do understand why you are."

Caroline listened to the sound of his voice. It was soft and apologetic. But, she noted there was something else. His voice shook. Suddenly, she wasn't afraid any more. With a half smile she nodded. Picking up the big spoon next to the stove, she carefully poured hot beans into bowls and placed them on the table.

"Then, we will pray, Mr. Cartwright. We don't have much but you are welcome to a bowl of beans and some potatoes."

The boys chattered on and on with James between bites; asking questions about the southern half of Arkansas. They had lived there when young, but that had been when Thomas was alive. They didn't remember what it looked like.

"You won't see mountains like this," James told them. "The land is flat where crops grow. The cotton plants get so tall you can't see a person on the other side. Yes sir, mighty fine land. Or, it was before the war. But, it will get there again. You wait and see."

"No mountains? How can there be no mountains?" Tommy asked.

"Well, the geography of Arkansas makes it where the mountains are up here and down where I came from the land is flatter. God made different kinds of places because we need farm land and we need mountains to break up the weather so the crops will grow better where the farms are."

"Oh," Tommy said with a nod of his head.

"Tommy really don't know what you are talking about, but I do. He's more interested in doing things with his hands. You know, create things," Timmy replied. "I might be going to the academy someday. Maw wants us to get a good education beyond what we can get here. She would like to send us as soon as we are old enough; that is, if the doors are opened again."

"If the doors are opened?" James asked with a frown.

Caroline steadily looked at the man. Again she narrowed her eyes.

"Yes, if the doors are ever opened again. The academy was burned to the ground during the war. Unscrupulous raiders burned it. Hopefully it's being rebuilt at this time, but I really doubt that it is. You didn't know that, Mr. Cartwright? Don't you think you should have found out before you traveled all this distance in the wintertime?"

James rubbed his scraggy whiskers. Looking around, he tried clearing his throat.

"I didn't know. I...I've been away. I've only been back in Arkansas for about four months. Like I said, I knew about the excellent academy in Mountain Home before the war. Someone from there had come down to Monticello and had mentioned it. I didn't know it had been burned."

"Where were you during the war, Mr. Cartwright? Did you see battle?" Caroline asked anxiously.

James gave a deep sigh. His hand began to shake. Pulling it beneath the table he looked at his lap. A lump filled his throat and a pain shot through his abdomen. Clearing his throat, he slowing moved his unsteady hand and wiped his mouth.

"If you don't mind I will take those blankets now and go to the shed. This was a delicious meal, Ma'am. I will try to find a way to repay you."

Caroline was puzzled by the man's reaction. She wanted to ask again, but refrained. Quietly she rose from the table and spoke to Tommy.

"Get Mr. Cartwright two blankets from the chest."

"Can't Timmy –"

"I told you to get them," Caroline sternly answered.

Tommy moved from the table and disappeared through a nearby door. Soon he was back with two wool blankets.

"Maw, it's really cold out there. Can't he sleep in here by the fire?"

"No, Tommy, he can't," she quickly answered. Turning to James, she added, "Mr. Cartwright, if you sleep in the hay you should be warm. I will send one of the boys out to fetch you in the morning for breakfast. After that, you can be on your way."

"Thank you, Mrs. Hollister," James replied as he took the blankets.

Walking to the door, the boys were at his heels.

"We'll be out there first thing in the morning," Timmy exclaimed. "Maybe you can tell us more about the flat lands before you leave."

James looked back at Caroline.

"We'll see, boys, we'll see," he answered. Turning toward the door, he reached for the handle.

"Mr. Cartwright, we don't have much here to steal. The bushwhackers didn't leave much in this area. I don't know why our house was spared but it was. Maybe it was because we live so far into the trees on the mountainside that it was possible they didn't bother with us after -," Caroline stopped and took a breath. "Just the same, the war took most of everything. We don't welcome strangers. The war may be over but there are still raiders everywhere. We have to be very careful."

James spun toward Caroline and shook his head.

"Ma'am, I'm not a thief or a killer and I'm not here to steal anything. I just need a place to sleep tonight. I'll...I'll pay you for your hospitality as soon as I can."

Caroline's eyes met his again. She could see sadness; a deep, burdened sadness. But there was also anger. She knew she had touched something deep inside of him. She wanted to turn her eyes away, but couldn't. Her eyes couldn't leave his.

Finally, she watched as he dropped his eyes and turned back to the door. Opening it, he took three steps to his right and ducked his head as the wind and cold took away his breath. Caroline shut the door behind him. Pulling the latch, she made sure the door was secure.

"Boys, it's time to get ready for bed. I'll tuck you in and pray with you when I get the dishes done."

Holding her shoulders, Caroline stared at the door. There was something… something about the man.

"Maw? Maw, did you hear me? I asked if I could have another piece of cornbread before I go to bed," Tommy said.

"What? Oh yes, you can have some more cornbread then it is off to bed."

Putting the last dish away, Caroline glanced out the window. She couldn't see the shed. The window had frosted. Darkness had taken over.

Lowering her head, she moved toward the bed in the corner of the room where the twins were waiting. Kneeling beside the bed, she smiled at the boys.

"Who wants to go first tonight?" she asked.

"I will go first," Tommy replied.

Putting his hands together, he closed his eyes and started to pray aloud.

"Lord, thank you for your love and protection. Thank you for the food we eat and the house we live in. Thank you for the war being over," Tommy prayed

"And, thank you for our mother. She works hard to keep us fed and clothed. Bless Granny and Grampa and our aunts and uncles and cousins. Also bless Mr. Cartwright. He looks like he needs friends," Timmy added.

"Yeah, and a bath," Tommy continued. "I like him and I hope you help him. He seems very nice. Make well those that are sick. Amen."

Caroline listened carefully to their words as each took a turn. When it was her turn she repeated the names of those her sons had asked help and healing for and then silently prayed for the man in the shed.

Saying amen, she carefully pulled the covers around the boys.

"Maw, why couldn't Mr. Cartwright sleep in the house?" Timmy asked.

"We don't know him, Timmy. He is a stranger and you know we have talked about not trusting strangers. You should have hurried out of the shed and told me about him being there instead of bringing him into the house."

"He was nice, Maw," Tommy answered, "And…and, he looked so lonely."

"And cold," Timmy chimed in. "The shed is so cold. Are you sure he is going to be all right out there?"

"Yes, he is going to be fine. If he was in the war, he probably slept in colder places than our shed. Now, boys it's time to go to sleep. Close your eyes and have pleasant dreams."

"I love you, Maw," the boys chorused.

"I love you, too. Stop talking and go to sleep."

Moving from the bed, Caroline stoked the fire and added another log before walking to her small bedroom and crossing to the dark window. She still could not see the shed. Darkness covered it. There was no moon.

"Lord, protect the animals out in the shed. Keep them all warm enough tonight." Caroline stopped for a moment and then continued in a softer voice. "Lord, protect Mr. Cartwright who is out in the building with the animals. Protect him and help him."

Having finished, she turned to the wicker chair and pulled her nightgown from the back. After changing, she slid under the blanket and quilt on the bed.

It seemed hours before she finally was able to close her eyes and fall into a troubled sleep.

CHAPTER 6

"Maw, Maw!" yelled Tommy as he ran into her bedroom.

Drowsily, Caroline opened her eyes. The window showed light.

"Maw, we must have two or three feet of snow!" Tommy exclaimed as Caroline came out of her room.

Hurriedly, she crossed the room and looked out. White covered everything. Nothing could be distinguished. Looking around, her eyes took in the sparkling ice speckled snow. Deep blue valleys lay between the humps of unrecognizable objects. Red birds hopped from one limb to another on the tree closest to the house.

"Boys, get dressed. I will get breakfast ready while you check on the animals."

"Do you want us to tell Mr. Cartwright breakfast will be ready soon?" Timmy asked as he pulled on his coat and cap.

"Mr. Cartwright! I forgot about him!" Caroline exclaimed as she turned and glanced out the frosty window once more. "Yes, yes, tell him it will be ready soon."

67

Caroline was just finishing the gravy when the door opened. The boys rushed in and pulled their boots and caps off. Hanging their coats on the nails by the door, they hurried to the fireplace.

"Where is Mr. Cartwright?" she asked, pulling biscuits from the oven.

"He'll be here in a few minutes," Tommy answered.

"Why do you get to tell her everything?" Timmy shouted. "I never get to tell her anything!"

"That's because you're too slow," Tommy exclaimed.

"Well, it's not fair," Timmy replied.

"Boys, stop! Listen to you. This is not the way brothers should talk to each other. Now, Timmy, look out the door to see if Mr. Cartwright is coming. The gravy will not stay hot forever."

Timmy moved from the hearth and started toward the door just as it opened.

"I'm sorry, I guess I should have knocked," James said as he stepped in.

"That's all right, Mr. Cartwright," Tommy answered. "We knew you were coming in."

"Tommy!" Carolina chastised.

"No, boys, it wasn't right. I should have knocked."

There was a scramble as the boys pushed and shoved their way into their chairs. Turning their heads, they waited for their mother to join them.

"You boys are getting more rowdy all the time! You need your f...." Stopping, Caroline looked at the table then cleared her throat. "You need to settle down. We have a guest at the table."

"Yes, ma'am," the boys chorused.

Bowing their heads, Caroline looked at James.

"Mr. Cartwright, would you like to say grace?" she asked.

James looked in her direction and then looked at the table.

"I...I think it best for you to say the prayer, ma'am. Thank you for asking just the same."

Caroline nodded and bowed her head again. "Lord, thank you for protecting us through the night and this morning. Please guide us today in all that we do. Lord, I thank you for the bounty you have given us. Bless the food we have for the health of our bodies. Amen."

Once the prayer was over, food was passed around the table and soon the plates were filled with biscuits and gravy.

"Maw, these are the bestest biscuits!" Tommy said, shoveling another mouthful in. "I like the jelly with the gravy. It makes it taste so good."

"Well, don't put too much jelly young man," his mother answered. "After you finish your gravy you can have another biscuit with jelly if you would like."

"I want my biscuit and gravy without jelly," Timmy put in shaking his head. "I like a biscuit with jelly but not with my gravy."

Caroline laughed and looked at James. He was smiling.

"I hope biscuits and gravy are all right with you this morning, Mr. Cartwright. This and oats are my sons' favorite breakfast."

"The food is fine, ma'am. It's been quite a while since I had food this good. Thank you for letting me stay and eat."

"Mister Cartwright, I hope you slept warm enough last night," Caroline cordially said after looking at him a few minutes. He was eating like he hadn't eaten in some time.

"It was fine, Mrs. Hollister. I snuggled up next to the cow and slept quite warm."

The boys laughed and pushed each other while pretending to cuddle up.

"Boys! What is wrong with you this morning? This is not the place to misbehave or the time. I am so sorry, Mr. Cartwright. They usually don't act this bad."

"That's all right, ma'am. Boys will be boys. I've seen worse behavior. It doesn't bother me," James answered, looking at the boys.

Both boys had lowered their heads and were cutting their eyes toward their mother. James wanted to laugh but knew it wouldn't be right.

"Well, it bothers me! You must apologize to Mr. Cartwright right now and then finish your breakfast!" Caroline said with disdain.

"Sorry," came the reply. Picking up forks, they started eating.

With breakfast over, the boys headed to the shed once again. Most of the chores were finished except for the milking. Grabbing the pail, Timmy handed it to Tommy.

"It's your turn," he said with a smirk.

"Why is it my turn?" Tommy asked back.

"I have milked the cow the last five times. You always seem to have an excuse so you can get out of it. This morning the chores are done already. Mr. Cartwright helped us out."

Timmy stopped and held up his hand. Counting on his fingers, he named the finished chores.

With a grimace, Tommy grabbed the pail in his gloved hand and started for the door.

James watched the interaction and then followed the boys toward the door.

"Thank you again, Mrs. Hollister, for your kindness and generosity. I will get my things ready and be on my way shortly. I'll tell the boys bye while they are out in the shed."

"I hope you find a job, Mr. Cartwright. It will be hard this time of year, but maybe you will find something you can do."

Nodding, James turned to the door and opened it.

Caroline stood and watched as the door closed behind him. Turning to the stove she picked up the pot of hot water and proceeded to the pan where the waiting dishes were stacked. Just as the last dish was finished, the door opened again.

"Everything is frozen!" Timmy yelled as he entered on a gust of wind.

"All the snow is under the ice!" Tommy exclaimed, with hands circling in the air.

"Maw, Mr. Cartwright can't leave in all the ice!" Timmy spoke out. "He will freeze!"

"Yeah, Maw, he can't leave! It's too cold and there is nothing but ice!" Tommy added. "His horse might fall down and Mr. Cartwright could be killed!"

Caroline dried her hands and walked to the door. The boys had to be exaggerating. There couldn't be that much ice.

As she got to Tommy, she noticed the frame of the front window was rimmed with ice. Motioning for him to put the milk on the cabinet, she continued to the door.

Wind hit her face as she opened it. The cold was intense and went through her clothes. Her eyes stung. Closing the door, she looked back into the room.

"Maw, Mr. Cartwright is leaving in a few minutes. Right now he is putting extra straw in the stalls for the animals so they won't freeze. Maw, are you going to let him leave?" Timmy asked.

Caroline looked at her son. His face was animated. He was logical. He always thought things through. Tommy, on the other hand, was always compulsive. He had been the one that invited the stranger into the house without thinking.

"Maw?" Timmy said again, "Maw, the bible said we are to help those that don't have as much as we do. Remember? Mr. Cartwright don't have food or a place to sleep. We have plenty to eat and a warm house. We should help him."

Caroline sighed and stared at the stove. She, too, remembered the scriptures Timmy had read only a week before.

Looking around she tried to think of an alternative answer, but couldn't. It would be warmer in the house. Not only did they have the stove but they had the fireplace. James Cartwright could sleep on the floor close to it.

Lord, this is crazy. I can't let the man leave with conditions like they are. I can't leave him outside where he might freeze to death. What would the boys think if something happened to him? But, can I let him stay in the house?

Turning to the boys, she wiped her hands on her apron again. With another long sigh, she shook her head.

"I can't believe I am saying this. I think I have completely gone insane for even considering such a thought, but all right, boys, go tell Mr. Cartwright to come into the house. Don't forget to bring in the blankets when you come back."

The boys jumped around the room and ran toward the door.

"Wait! Get your coats and boots on! You don't need to catch a cold."

Laughing, they hurried into their boots, coats, caps, and gloves and ran toward the shed. Slipping and sliding, they whooped and hollered all the way as they held the rope.

Soon, the door opened again and James stood just inside the threshold.

"Are you sure, Mrs. Hollister?" his voice weakly asked.

"I'm sure, Mr. Cartwright, but this is only temporary. As soon as the ice is gone, you will need to move on. Is that understood?"

Caroline could feel her neck stretching high. Her face was drawn and uncomfortable.

"Yes, ma'am, I understand. When you say it is time to leave, I will go," James answered, eyes steady on Caroline's face.

Looking around the room, Caroline tried to calm herself. She couldn't look in his direction.

"You...you will have to sleep on the floor. I don't have any other room."

"The floor is fine, Mrs. Hollister. I can sleep almost anywhere. I appreciate your hospitality."

Finally, Caroline looked at James. His face was white. There wasn't much muscle under the drooping sleeves of his shirt. His belt had several new notches where it buckled.

"Mr. Cartwright, there is one thing. I know this is the Lord's day, but you need a bath."

The twins began to giggle. Caroline turned to them and frowned. They quickly stopped and looked at the floor.

"You and the boys can bring in water that I will heat. If you can't get water, then bring in snow. Do you have extra clothes?"

Her mind was running through the chest in her bedroom. She knew she had tucked away two of Thomas's shirts and a pair of pants after she had gotten the letter of his death. They would probably fit this man.

James's eyes widened. Swallowing hard, he looked down at his appearance. He hadn't realized how bad he looked. He imagined how much worse his smell must be after sleeping with the cow and his horse.

"Yes, ma'am, I have another shirt and pants in my bag. I was saving them for... for the academy."

"You can put those clothes on and I will wash the clothes you have on and dry them close to the fire. You can take the bath after we eat breakfast."

"We'll help get snow after breakfast, Maw!" the boys chorused.

"That's going to be a lot of snow," she answered.

"We don't mind!" Tommy answered with a giggle. He punched Timmy in the ribs.

As the boys and James finished eating, they started getting ready to go outside. Caroline pulled Timmy aside and got close enough to whisper.

"You need to go to your grandparents' cabin and tell them we will not be over because of the weather. We will do our bible study here. Don't forget to ask if they need anything. It may be a few days before we get out."

"Yes, ma'am," Timmy answered, wrapping his woolen scarf around his neck.

Caroline waited in her bedroom while James used the tub in the kitchen. The boys sat on the bed as she read to them from the bible. They sunk deep into the feather mattress. Occasionally she stopped and listened to see if there was a knock on the door.

She was on a fourth chapter when the knock came. The boys quickly jumped off the bed and opened the door.

"We thought we were going to freeze before you got out of the tub!" Tommy yelled as he passed James and headed to the fireplace.

"We weren't freezing," Timmy said as he rolled his eyes.

Caroline stared. The man before her was clean shaven and smelled of the lye soap she had given him. His clothes were clean but hung on his thin frame.

"I'm sorry I took so long," he apologized. Looking down, he pulled on both sides of his pants. "I guess I lost a little weight since I wore these last."

"No, no don't apologize. You needed your privacy to bathe. The boys and I didn't mind." Stopping for a moment, she looked at him again. "Your clothes are a little big but you look all right."

"And, me and my clothes look clean," James answered with a laugh. "I hadn't realized how awful I must have looked. Thank you for letting me clean up in your kitchen. I've already taken the water out and wiped the floor."

"I bet it was black!" Tommy yelled as he rubbed his hands on his warming behind.

"Tommy! That is not polite, young man! Apologize!"

Tommy looked at the floor and rubbed his socked foot across it.

"That's all right, ma'am," James said as he turned to Tommy. "Yes, the water was pretty black. That's why I got rid of it before anyone could see it."

"I bet it was so black it turned the ice and snow black!"

Everyone laughed except Caroline. She was upset with the boys' behavior. She knew there was more they needed to learn.

"Mrs. Hollister, I haven't taken offense to what the boys are saying. They are just boys. Don't worry about it. I'm not," James said, almost as though he had read her mind.

"Thank you," Caroline quietly said to James after the boys sat down at the table. "Would you like another cup of coffee?"

"I would love it," he replied with a smile.

"Boys, since we have already read our bible verses this morning you can play some games. Mind you, play nice and don't be fighting."

"But what about a story? Granny always tells a story," Tommy whined.

"Tommy, we can go one Sunday without a story," Caroline chided. "Don't worry about it."

Tommy tightened his lips and looked at the floor. As he started to walk toward the rug, Timmy ran in front of him.

"We can do a story!" he yelled. "We can do the one about helping the Samaritan when he got beat up and robbed!"

Tommy's smile was so large it hurt his face.

"I know that one! We can act it out like Granny!"

After pouring the coffee, Caroline handed it to the man in front of the fireplace. Sitting down in her rocking chair, she nodded at the boys.

"All right, I think that is a wonderful idea. We will sit here and listen," she told them.

The boys stood in front of the hearth and began telling the story. Tommy was the man who was robbed and beaten and Timmy was the Good Samaritan.

Laughing, Caroline and James watched as Tommy punched at the air and pretended to be losing an imaginary battle. Once on the floor, Timmy walked by and then helped his brother to his feet and carried him toward the rug. The story was finished when Timmy announced that he would pay for the man to be helped.

"The moral of the story," Timmy said, "is that we should help those who have lost everything."

Caroline lowered her head and wet her lips. She wondered if the boys had done that particular story because of the circumstance that was at hand.

Raising her head she smiled at the boys. "That was very graphic, boys. I really enjoyed it. Thank you for doing the story. You will have to do it again when we go to your granny's home. Now, I have to get dinner ready. We will have a variety of foods since I didn't expect to be eating here. But, that will be all right."

After the meal, Caroline told the boys to play games on the rug. She poured a cup of coffee and took it to James.

"How is it that you found our shed, Mr. Cartwright? There is a cabin in the hollow before you get to this one. Why did you not go in their shed or knock on their door?

James looked at his coffee. Shaking his head he looked up.

"I...I don't know. It was dark and snowing. I don't know how I missed another cabin. I can't explain it, ma'am."

Caroline's eyes narrowed but she held her tongue. She could feel something in this man... something she wasn't completely sure of...but she didn't want to believe he was a liar.

Turning away, Caroline stared at the logs aflame in the fireplace. Thoughts flew through her mind. She wanted to know more about this man who was also staring into the flames.

Opening her mouth, she started to speak. Something stopped her. Something changed in the man's demeanor. She realized it wasn't the time to ask questions about the past.

Looking more closely she could see a tiny tear in the corner of the man's eye. Moving her eyes down to his hands, she watched as he rubbed his wrists over and over. She could see dark circles around the wrists. Slowly, he began to rub his hands together. His knuckles began to turn white.

His body is here, she thought, *but he isn't.*

"Are you all right, Mr. Cartwright?" she slowly asked with a wrinkle across her forehead.

James sat up straight and looked around. Clearing his throat, his jaw line moved. He could feel and hear the grind of his teeth. Swallowing, he lowered his head again and nodded.

"I'm fine, Mrs. Hollister. I...I guess I was in the past. It...it wasn't good. I'm sorry."

"Don't be, Mr. Cartwright. You must have lived through some horrible experiences. If...if you would like to talk about them, I am here."

Nodding, James stared once again into the fire, but said nothing.

CHAPTER 7

Sunday afternoon passed with little conversation. James and the boys checked on the animals and then ate a supper of boiled cabbage and cornbread.

"Are you sure this is enough?" Caroline asked looking at the almost bare table.

James winked at the boys. "This and a piece of the cobbler you baked will be plenty. In fact, I don't know about the boys, but I could eat just the cobbler."

"Yeah," Tommy echoed.

"No, you will eat something before you get cobbler," Caroline sternly said to her son.

It was hard getting the boys into bed. They continued to be excited. When they were finally settled, Caroline pointed at the blankets that had been brought in from the shed.

"I have a pillow I will bring you. I'm afraid this is the best I can do."

"This is just fine, Mrs. Hollister. In fact, it is almost like sleeping in a palace. Thank you."

Caroline kept looking back at the man sitting near the hearth as she went to get him a pillow. Many questions filled her head but she knew they could wait. Wait until another time.

"I...I think I will go to bed now, Mr. Cartwright. I sleep lightly. That means I hear every sound in the house," Caroline began as she handed him the pillow.

"Don't worry, Mrs. Hollister. I'm going outside for a moment and then I will be settling right here on the floor for the night. I won't be wondering around if that's what you are afraid of."

"I...I," Caroline closed her mouth, nodded, and turned toward the kitchen. Quickly, she moved toward her little room in the back.

Sunlight was coming through the tiny window when Caroline awakened. Hurriedly she changed and headed toward the door between her room and the kitchen. The checkerboard was set up on the table. The boys were scratching their heads and concentrating on their next moves. James watched and nodded from time to time.

Tommy's hand hovered over a checker and then he glanced up at the man watching them. The man gave a slight nod and the boy moved the piece. Caroline watched this happen several times.

As his brother scratched his head, Tommy smiled with satisfaction. He had made a good move.

"I am so sorry for getting up so late!" she said as she scurried toward the pan to wash her face and hands.

"No problem," James answered.

"Yeah, Maw," Tommy agreed without looking up. "We already et."

"You have? What did you eat?"

"We ate cold biscuits, butter, and syrup. Boy was it good!" Timmy said, frowning. He was still trying to figure out how Tommy was making such good moves.

"Well, then the animals – "

"Already been taken care of," James answered with a smile. "Milk is setting right there on the cupboard."

Caroline stared at the milk and shook her head.

"Well, I guess I'll eat something and then put up the milk," she replied with raised brows.

Looking around, she noticed no one was paying attention to her. They were absorbed in the game. An hour later, they were still playing checkers, but now with vengeance. Timmy couldn't let his brother take control of the games.

Caroline knitted on the blanket she was making Timmy for Christmas. It was almost finished. Just a few more rows and it would join Tommy's in the chest in her bedroom. Warm woolen socks were already there along with a new pair of britches and a shirt for each boy.

Grimacing, Caroline continued her work. There wouldn't be anything special again this year. The war had taken everything. There had been only enough money to buy necessities and now that money was gone. If she couldn't meet the peddler soon and barter with him for some of the handmade items she had done, she wouldn't be able to get the new boots they needed. She had planned to give them as Christmas presents.

She looked at the boys and shook her head. If they were on the plantation, she could go into town and buy the boots herself. She wouldn't have to worry if the peddler remembered the request she had asked Thom to give him. She didn't even know if he would get the boots and have them on his wagon. She didn't like having to wait weeks to see if he could bring items they needed.

With a sigh, she looked back at her crochet. At least the farm was self-sustaining. Her father-in-law had put up sorghum and killed a hog for her. They had grown grain for the flour and the garden had produced well. There was cornmeal and canned vegetables along with dried fruit. They had even found an old hollow tree where bees had taken up residence. The boys wanted to get the honey but she had held them back while her brother-in-law and his father had cleaned the comb out of the tree.

The cotton patch had produced enough cotton that she and her mother-in-law had made clothes for the winter. Her in-laws sheep had also been shorn and the wool had been spun into yarn for socks and long johns.

"If only I could grow coffee," she whispered. "I hate waiting on the peddler for coffee."

"I won, Maw! I won against Timmy! Can you believe it! I won three games out of five!" Tommy shrieked.

"It won't happen again," Timmy quietly remarked.

Tommy looked up at James and winked at him. "I wouldn't be too sure."

James patted both boys on the head and smiled.

"Boys, you need to check on the animals and make sure they are all right," Caroline said, while putting away the crochet. "Make sure the water isn't frozen. They need to be able to get water."

"Yes, ma'am," they answered in unison.

"I'll go out with them, Mrs. Hollister. I need to stretch my legs," James said, grabbing his worn coat and hat.

Caroline looked at the coat.

"Mr. Cartwright, I have a coat you can wear. It will be warmer than the one you have. Wait a moment and I will get it."

Going to her room, Caroline hesitated in front of her cedar chest that filled a corner of the room. With a quick move, she opened the chest and moved several things around. Pulling out a red checkered coat, she closed the lid and returned to the front room.

She looked pale as she handed the coat to James.

"This…this will be warmer, Mr. Cartwright," she said as she placed it in his hand. Quickly, she turned away. She didn't want him to see the tears that glistened.

Caroline busied herself with makings for bread. The morning had gotten away from her. She wanted to make loaves to last a few days.

She had the bread dough rising and a pie made before she realized the boys had not returned from the barn. Wiping her hands, she stepped to the door and looked out.

The wind whipped her hair. Cold crept into her clothing and she began to chill. Walking to the porch and steps, she looked all around.

"Boys?" she called, pulling her shawl closed.

No answer. Frowning, she strained to listen. The only sound she heard was toward the woods. A constant whack, whack came from her left.

"Boys!" she yelled.

Tommy came running from the edge of the woods. Waving, he yelled back.

"We're cutting wood, Maw! We'll soon be back in the house. We're almost finished."

Suddenly, Caroline saw James and Timmy emerge from the trees. A sled of wood trailed behind them.

With relief Caroline waved, walked back into the dog-run, and closed the door behind her. Leaning against the door, she sighed.

The boys were safe. No harm had befallen them.

Straightening, she thought of James Cartwright. Anger filled her.

"He should know better than take them out there without letting me know," she spoke into the air. "I will have to let him know this can't happen again."

When the door finally opened, the boys rushed in. Their boots were ice and snow covered.

"I didn't mean to have the boys out there, Mrs. Hollister," James said as he hung his coat on a peg. "I saw the woodpile was getting low so I grabbed the axe and went out to cut some wood. I didn't know they followed me."

Caroline ran her tongue across her teeth. Her anger was fading.

"Next time, Mr. Cartwright, have one of the boys come back and tell me. I was worried."

"Yes, ma'am," James replied with a smile. Winking at the boys, he pulled his boots off and placed them by the door.

The boys followed his lead.

"I like the way he cuts wood, Maw," Tommy said as he flopped into a chair. "It don't take him no time to fell a tree and get it cut up. It's not like when you do it. We didn't have to stand around and wait for him to finish."

"Yes, and he showed us a way to hold the axe so we get the maximum cut with it. Wait until you see how we can cut wood! We can cut it from now on. You won't even have to help us," Timmy chimed in.

"And, we can cut wood for Grampa and Granny!" Tommy added.

Caroline sighed and nodded.

Sadness filled her. The boys were growing up. They weren't her babies anymore. First they helped in the fields and now they were chopping wood. She didn't have to hover over them anymore.

"Your britches' legs are wet," she finally could get out over the lump in her throat. "Stand by the hearth and warm yourself. I don't want the two of you to catch a death of cold. I'll make you something warm to drink."

"Mr. Cartwright needs to warm up, too," Timmy replied.

Caroline looked at James and nodded.

"I'll make a pot of coffee, too," she answered.

James watched the flames flicker and lick the logs. He looked around the room and at the ceiling and floor.

The house was well made. The logs were tight. The chinking was secure. The plank floor was well built and hewn perfectly to a slick seal.

The only thing he didn't like was the way the wind whistled through the rafters of the attic. If he could have access to the area, he could chink and plaster so the wind couldn't go through. Then it wouldn't be as cold and the boys....

Caroline's presence, more than the outstretched hand, drew his attention.

"I couldn't remember if you put milk in your coffee this morning," she apologized.

"Black is how I drink it," he quickly answered.

Wrapping his fingers around the cup, he looked around to see where the boys were. They had returned to the kitchen table and were playing a card game. Quietly, he turned back toward the fire.

"I learned to drink coffee during the war. We had to stay alert. Coffee kept us awake."

"Were you here or in the East, Mr. Cartwright?" Caroline asked as she sat down next to him.

James struggled with his thoughts for a moment then turned to Caroline.

"I was back East, Mrs. Hollister. The war...the fighting takes the life out of a man. Death...," James stopped and shook his head. He looked into the fire again and sipped the coffee.

Caroline opened her mouth but the boys hurried to her side.

"Maw, I caught Tommy cheating!" Timmy exclaimed.

"I wasn't cheating!" Tommy screeched. "I just accidentally dropped some cards and he thought I was!"

"I'm going to finish making bread, so I will be right there watching from now on. You boys need to learn to get along. It may be a long winter."

Caroline could see James was lost in thought. She wanted to ask more about what had happened during the war but knew it would have to wait.

"Maw, do you want us to check on Granny and Grampa? We can feed and water their animals," Timmy finally asked.

"What? Oh!"

Caroline quickly looked out the front window. Smoke was coming from the chimney of a log cabin about a hundred yards away.

"I think they are okay. They have a good fire going, so I know they are warm. Wait, I can see your grandfather coming out of the woods. He's been to the shed."

James froze for a moment. His eyes widened and his head rose higher above his shoulders.

What did the woman say? The man was coming out of the shed? What if he found....

James frowned and dropped his head again. He would have to face the consequences if he did.

Caroline didn't see his reaction. She was busy looking out the window. She watched as the older man carefully moved from the dense forest on the hillside and quickly stepped toward the house. She noticed he stopped, stamped his feet, and looked toward her house.

Hurrying to the porch, she waved at him. She watched as he waved back and turned toward his house again. Closing the door after entering, she walked back to the pie safe.

"They are fine, boys. I don't think they need you to go over and help. Not at this time anyway. Maybe tomorrow if this weather continues."

James got up and walked to the small front window. Looking out, he saw an old, gray log cabin standing near the woods at the base of the hill. He hadn't seen it when he came into the hollow. It was hidden by the dense wooded land around it.

His eyes widened.

What if he had gone to that house first? Would he have been let in?

"That house belongs to my husband's parents," Caroline said behind him.

"Have they lived there a long time?" James asked without taking his eyes off the cabin.

"This land has been in Thomas's family for two generations. Thomas made the third. The cabin was built by Thomas's father and grandfather."

James looked around the land that lay beyond the window. It was a narrow valley between two hills. A small stream flowed through it and supplied the water that was used by both houses.

"I'm surprised the stream hasn't frozen," he said.

"It is spring fed. We have water year round. I'm glad of that. The spring is in a little hollow on the side of the hill where it is hidden from view. The water is clear and warm."

James nodded and looked at the older cabin again. He could only pray the man didn't find his horse and blanket roll when he was in the shed.

Moving to the stove, he poured another cup of coffee and proceeded back to the chair by the fire.

Caroline looked out the window again and then joined him.

"I'm surprised Thom hasn't been over to check on us. He usually comes over often."

James continued to stare at nothing in particular, taking a sip of coffee now and then.

Caroline blushed, suddenly aware of how awkward it was to have a man in the house.

James felt the change. Looking in her direction, he saw her face pale. Realization hit him.

"I...I'm sorry, I just realized. You must think me callous and insensitive. Forgive me, Mrs. Hollister. If you are uncomfortable because of my presence in the house, I can leave. I don't want to cause a problem with your in-laws."

Caroline's eyes grew wide and finally settled back to normal after several blinks.

"No, no, that is fine, Mr. Cartwright. I said you could stay in the house for now. It is bitterly cold out. I'm sure they will understand under the circumstances."

Clearing her throat, Caroline got up and returned to the kitchen to check on the rising bread dough.

Would her in-laws understand?

Chapter 8

The house was quiet. Caroline peered out her bedroom window but couldn't see any movements.

Her eyes searched for the red jackets of her boys but there was no sign of them.

"Maybe they are behind the shed already," she said to herself.

Slowly, she moved to the front room and checked the wood in the fireplace.

Quiet, whiskered, Millie stretched and moved around the room.

"You want outside for awhile?" Caroline asked as she picked up the yellow tabby cat. "There might be a mouse in the corn crib."

Opening the door, she watched as the cat crossed the melting ice. Just as she turned from the door a knock jarred her and she did an about face just as it opened.

"Hope I didn't scare you, Caroline. Sarah thought I needed to get my britches over here to check on you and the boys. We been hearing some gunshots lately." A tired, weather-worn man said from the doorway.

"Thom, you did scare me," Caroline said with relief. "Come in and warm yourself. I'll make some coffee."

"Where's them boys? I figured they would be jumpin' all over me by now," Thom Hollister said as he sat down at the table.

"They are hunting with Mr. Cartwright," Caroline answered. Suddenly, she stopped.

"Mr. Cartwright? Who is Mr. Cartwright? Is he the one that's been shootin'? Is that his horse I saw in your shed yesterday?" Thom said with a stern look. "Caroline is there –"

Caroline's face flushed as she turned toward Thom and gave a sigh. She knew she would some explaining to do. Before Thom could finish his sentence and she could reply, the door opened.

"Maw, we got four squirrels and a turkey!" Tommy exclaimed. "I shot one of the squirrels myself! Grampa, come see the squirrel I killed!"

Caroline stood motionless. Thom got up from the table and put his hat back on his head. Turning, he gave her a strange look and then followed Tommy to the door.

"Well, let's see what the new hunter has killed," he replied. "Caroline, you keep that coffee hot. I'll be back in. Maybe we need to talk. Seems something is going on."

"Yes, Thom," she quietly answered.

Watching from the door, she listened as Tommy explained that Timmy had also killed a squirrel.

It seemed like an eternity before the door finally opened. Caroline had rehearsed over and over her explanation of why James Cartwright was at her house. She was nervous. She didn't know how Thomas's father would respond to another man being there with her and the boys.

"I want my squirrel for supper!" Tommy was yelling as he came through the door. "Timmy wants his, too. Can we have them for supper, Maw?"

Timmy was two steps behind his brother with a skinned squirrel in each of his bloody hands.

"Yes, yes, of course," Caroline answered. "You boys put the squirrels in that bowl on the table and then scrub your hands."

She watched and waited for the men to come in. They didn't.

"Where...where is Grampa Thom and Mr. Cartwright?" she asked uneasily.

"Oh, they're still in the shed," Timmy replied, "They're talking."

Wringing her hands, Caroline sat at the table. Another hour passed.

What are they talking about? She wondered.

The door opened suddenly and two solemn men came through. The men joined Caroline in the kitchen.

"I hope you don't mind a skinned turkey," James said. "I didn't know if you wanted to mess with turkey feathers since you had company."

"I —"

"Is that coffee still hot?" Thom asked. "I'm freezing and sure could use a cup."

Caroline cocked her head. She watched as James took off his coat and then washed his hands. He came around her and sat down across from Thom.

"I'll check," was all that Caroline could manage to get out as she backed away.

Busying herself with the coffee, she listened to the men talking.

"You'll have to come over some morning and we can try for some big game," Thom was saying. "The deer are fat and if we're lucky we might even be able to get a bear in the spring."

"A bear!" the boys squealed. "Grampa, you kill bears?"

"Of course, I do. I don't like them in my hog pen in the spring. They git my piglets. I need someone to help me get rid of them pesky things."

Caroline almost dropped the coffee cups.

Spring? Thom was talking about Mr. Cartwright hunting bear with him in the spring?

"I appreciate the offer, Mr. Hollister, but I'm not sure where I will be in the spring. I'll have to be hunting a job as soon as I can. If there are no teaching positions in Mountain Home, I will have to move on somewhere else. I may even go back south. There might be some positions available soon."

Thom stretched and sipped his coffee.

"I don't know. All them Yankee soldiers being stationed here in Arkansas will still put a great strain on us. I'm just glad I'm up here in the mountains instead of down where the plantations used to be. You might not even have land left after they get through with you."

James felt a pain go through his stomach. His fields were already gone. Nothing was growing. It would take time for the land to be re-established and profitable. He didn't believe in slavery and had paid his free Negroes well. Without the Negroes, it could take years to reestablish the farm. The only hope would be to get them to share-crop on the land and share in the profits. He didn't know if that would happen. The last he heard his workers were in Helena. They had followed the feds there after the soldiers had burned the fields.

"The offer still stands, young man, that I gave earlier," Thom said as he picked up his coffee again. "We will need teachers up here now that our men folk are back from the war. I don't think all of them will want to go back to farming. Towns will start to grow with the families moving to them and all. We'll need schools, for sure. There's a passel of young'ns living in these mountains."

With the cup empty, Thom got up from his chair.

"Mighty fine coffee, Caroline. I appreciate you warming me up. By the way, Sarah wants to know if you still plan to eat Christmas dinner over at our place."

"Yes, yes, we are." Caroline answered.

"James, I hope you can join us, too. We don't have much but what we have we are blessed when we can share it. Boys, I have to be going. Your granny will be watching for me."

"Grampa, we can have the turkey to eat! I bet Maw can cook it up real good," Tommy yelled as he jumped up from the floor.

Everyone laughed and Thom smoothed his grandson's hair.

"I think by Christmas that bird would be a mite old," he remarked. "We might have another one by then. If not, then we will be blessed to have a good ham to eat. Now, give me a great big hug. With this kind of weather, I might not git another one for awhile."

The twins hugged their grandfather and went back to the checkers' game they had started on the rug.

Caroline walked Thom to the door and waited for him to step outside.

"I think you should have said something about that man being here," he quietly chastised. "But, now that I've met him, I can see why you let him stay. I guess I'm glad he can help with the wood and animals. I'm sorry I haven't been able to get over here sooner."

"I...I thought for sure Timmy would tell you he was here when I sent him over to tell you we wouldn't be there for Sunday studies. I really worried why you didn't come over then. I'm sorry, Thom. I hope you forgive me."

"I do forgive you, dear girl. But be more careful from now on. Others might not be like him."

Caroline waved as Thom turned and went down the steps and carefully followed the icy path toward his home. Closing the door, she could hear James and the boys talking.

"So, Tommy, you got your father's and grandfather's name," James said, squatting near the boys.

"We both did!" Timmy answered. "Their names are Timothy Thomas Hollister. I got Timothy and he got Thomas. Our middle names are from our other grandpa. His name is Arthur James Locke."

"Yeah, so I am Thomas Arthur and he is Timothy James," Tommy chimed in.

"Do you two always finish what the other starts to say?" James asked, laughing.

"Always!" they answered in unison.

The frying squirrels filled the house with their aroma. The house was peacefully quiet but there was an underlying feeling of apprehension.

Caroline was glad the boys and James were checking the animals and the cat was sleeping next to the hearth. Her stomach was queasy and tightness filled it. She wasn't sure she could control her emotions.

Finally, she put her hands to her face.

Dear Lord, I didn't expect Thom to be so friendly with Mr. Cartwright. I didn't expect him to invite him to Christmas dinner. I don't know what to do. I've asked him to leave but now, now I wonder. He's keeping me in firewood and meat. The boys are learning so much from him. Am I disrespecting Thomas by letting him stay through the cold? Should I tell him the ice is almost gone and he needs to leave? Should I talk to Thom first?

Turning the squirrels, Caroline glanced out the window. The boys were grabbing James and trying to throw him on the ground. They were laughing, running, and squealing.

"They need a father," slipped out of Caroline's mouth. Putting her hand over her mouth, she groaned.

Caroline remained quiet throughout supper and into the evening. She was hurting inside.

As she put the boys to bed, Timmy hugged her.

"It's all right, Maw," he said with a smile. "We like Mr. Cartwright, too. Grampa even likes him. He thanked him for cutting firewood and killing the animals for us to eat. Grampa said he was glad he was here during the storm, too. Please let him stay. Winter's not over yet. We might have more freezes."

Caroline smoothed Timmy's hair.

"You are wise beyond your years, young man. How did you know I was worried about how your grandfather felt about Mr. Cartwright being here?"

"I could see it in your face. Tommy couldn't because his mind is too busy thinking all the time. I think Mr. Cartwright could see it. He has been quiet, too. Maybe you should talk to him."

"Maybe I should,' Caroline answered with a smile. "Now, my wonderful, wise son, you need to go to sleep. I will see you in the morning."

Caroline picked up her knitting when she returned to her rocking chair near the fireplace. James was watching the flames in the fire.

"I will be leaving soon," he quietly said. "The ice is clearing and there is no reason for me to stay."

Caroline's eyes grew large.

"But…but, my in-laws invited you to Christmas dinner. That's only a couple of weeks away. What would Thom think?"

"I don't want to horn in on your family, Mrs. Hollister. Those are your husband's parents. I really don't know if they would be comfortable with me there. I think Mr. Hollister was asking out of courtesy. I don't think he really meant it."

"Thom would not have invited you to come if he didn't mean it. And…and what about the boys? They will be expecting you to go. They are excited about Christmas."

James gazed at Caroline. His arms wanted to grab her and hold her. His heart wanted to spill out what it felt. But, he refrained.

How can I tell you I love you? He thought. *How can I explain that you saved my life?*

"How do you feel about me going, Mrs. Hollister? How would it feel to have a stranger in your in-laws home for Christmas?"

"I...," Caroline hesitated. "I don't know just yet how I will feel, Mr. Cartwright. All I know is that my father-in-law asked you to join us for dinner."

Caroline gritted her teeth. Pain was in her chest. A lump had formed in her throat.

"What about the weather?" James asked. "You asked me to leave when the weather cleared. It has cleared. There are patches of snow and ice left but I'm sure the road into the nearest town has thawed."

"There isn't a town close by, Mr. Cartwright. There is a settlement called Locust Grove a few miles away to the east but it would take some time to get there. What...what if we have another ice storm? Where will you go? There's no work in the middle of winter. There are no local schools and I'm sure the school hasn't been rebuilt completely yet in Mountain Home."

"I can always find a barn to sleep in or a porch to get under. I will survive."

Caroline stopped and looked around the room. Her insides were shaking. She didn't want to admit she needed him there. She wanted him there. She....

"I don't have any money, Mr. Cartwright. I can't give you anything but a roof over your head and food to eat in payment for you helping around here this winter. I…I don't even have a bed for you to sleep in." Caroline looked around the room wringing her hands. "If my in-laws approve, will you stay?"

James watched her closely. He could see the turmoil in her posture and in her eyes. He watched the movement of her hands.

Caroline finally looked in his direction again. Their eyes met.

"The boys are learning so much from you. They need to learn how to shoot and clean the animals we eat. They need to know how to cut wood and do repairs. I…I can't teach them those things. They…they… would miss you if you left."

James heart was beating fast. Joy was exploding inside.

"Then, I will stay if your in-laws agree to it. We'll see how things work out day by day. I don't want…," he took a deep breath, "I don't want you to feel uncomfortable. I will leave when you say."

Chapter 9

Clear skies and bright sunshine melted the snow and ice that plagued the little valley for days.

The house was quiet. Even the cat didn't want to be inside. She moved from the front window to the back window and then returned with a loud meow.

"What's the matter with you?" Caroline asked as she picked up the cat. "You tired of the house? You want to go outside where you can catch a big, juicy mouse?"

Finally, after petting the cat she slowly opened the door. The cat bounded from her arms and ran outside to explore.

Caroline tried to sew but kept sticking her fingers. Finally, she got up from her chair, moved to the door, and stepped into the dog-run.

Craning her neck, she poked it out a smidgen and let her eyes peer around the woods and up toward the hill. Noise filled the air. Birds were chirping in all directions. Fluttering wings and shadows played through the branches. There were no other movements.

Caroline had hoped to get a glimpse of the boys. They were hunting with James again. Both had taken to the woods with such enthusiasm that it was hard to keep them bottled up inside when snow wasn't falling.

"Well, Timmy, you were right. Tommy has taken to the woods. But, you were wrong also. It looks like you have taken to the woods along with him."

Laughing, she looked around again. Suddenly a shot rang out. There was a flutter of wings flying through the trees then quietness filled the air. Caroline listened, but there were no other sounds. No more shots.

Stepping back into the cabin, she said a small prayer that all was well on the side of the mountain.

Picking up paper and pen, she sat down at the table and began to write a letter to her mother. Sighing, she put the pen down and wiped her face.

"Mother, how do I explain to you that the boys are hunting with a man that is living in my house? *In my house?* I don't think you will understand," Caroline spoke aloud, shaking her head.

Picking the pen up again, she decided not to mention who the boys were hunting with. It would be easier that way. Her mother would think it would be Thom or one of the boys' uncles.

Placing the letter in an envelope, Caroline put the letter on the mantle. She didn't know when Thom would be able to mail it.

Turning around, her eyes fell on James's quilts and bag in the corner by the hearth. Looking around the room, she quietly moved toward them.

The quilts were lumpy. Slowly she picked one up and saw the round drum of a banjo. The cover was stretched tight and made of some animal's tanned hide. Cocking her head, she looked at it for several minutes. She wondered if the man played. He hadn't offered to get it out.

Looking back at the door, she again turned her attention to the leather bag next to the quilts. Humming, she started to pull the latch on the side.

"No, I can't do that!" she scolded herself. "Those things are private. I wouldn't want anyone looking in my bag if I was traveling."

Caroline covered the banjo with the quilt she had pulled away and then quickly moved back to the kitchen table.

"Lord, forgive me for being nosy. I shouldn't have even thought about looking in his bag!"

Shadows were growing long when the boys returned to the cabin.

"Look, Maw, we killed enough squirrels for supper!" Tommy yelled as he entered. "Everyone can have a whole one!"

"You don't have to shout for me to hear you," she quietly answered.

"We already have them cleaned, too," Timmy added in a calmer voice. "Mr. Cartwright showed us how to field dress them."

Caroline looked at the four big squirrels. She knew they were big red squirrels even though they had been skinned and gutted.

"It wasn't hard!" Tommy loudly agreed. "I love hunting with Mr. Cartwright! If I had my own knife, he wouldn't have to do all the work. I could help!"

"Well, you don't have a knife. And, you won't have one for quite a while. They are dangerous."

Getting up from the table, Caroline motioned for the boys to put the squirrels in a bowl. She could almost taste the stringent smell of fresh blood and meat.

"It looks like you boys have learned how to hunt very well," she said with a smile.

"We have!" exclaimed Timmy. "We could kill more squirrels if Tommy could sit still."

"I sit still!" Tommy refuted. "I just get cramped in my legs that's all. That can happen to you too!"

"Boys, that's enough. Let's not argue about who can sit still. It looks like both of you do a good job. You brought in squirrels to eat and that is what is important. Now wash the blood off your hands."

Getting up from the table, Caroline washed the squirrels and held them over a burner while the loose hairs burned away. Quietly, she got out flour and salt. Looking at the squirrels, she smiled. They would make a good meal with gravy.

"Where is Mr. Cartwright?" she finally asked. Thoughts of what she had almost done earlier disturbed her.

"He stopped at the shed. He said he would check on the animals before he comes in," Timmy answered, placing his hands in the cool soapy water his mother had made for him and Tommy.

Nodding, Caroline began preparing the squirrels for cooking.

"You should have seen me shoot the squirrel!" Timmy said.

"I did it better than you!" Tommy countered.

Caroline half listened as the boys continued to bicker over who was the better hunter. Her mind was on the banjo under the quilt.

James came through the door with two eggs in his hand.

"These were hidden in a stack of hay in the corner of the shed. I guess one of the hens has decided to lay in there instead of the hen house," he said with a grin.

"I'll put them away," Caroline answered. "Supper is almost ready. Would you like a cup of coffee while you wait?"

"That sounds wonderful! It's still cold out there and a cup of coffee will help warm me up."

James took the coffee and proceeded to the chair near the fireplace. Puzzled, he sat down and stared at the quilts. They didn't seem the same as when he left that morning. Looking over at the bag, he noticed it too had been moved.

Glancing toward Caroline, he lowered his brows for a moment.

Had she looked through his stuff?

Sighing, he took a sip of coffee.

There wasn't anything to see. The bag contained his other change of clothes and what papers he had. The important papers were in the leather pouch in the shed.

Supper was quiet. Caroline couldn't control her guilt. It ate at her.

"We need to eat squirrel and gravy every night!" Timmy spoke out.

"Yes, especially if we get to kill the squirrels!" Tommy answered, his mouth full.

"Boys, don't talk with food in your mouth," their mother scolded.

James continued to be quiet. His heart was sinking.

What if Caroline Hollister decided to look in the shed? What if she found the bedroll and its contents?

James shuttered.

Sitting near the fire, Caroline watched the flames flicker. Finally, she looked around and saw the boys busy looking at an old book with guns, knives, and other items that could be ordered.

Turning back to James she sighed and then looked at him.

"Mr. Cartwright, I owe you an apology. I…I picked up one of the quilts and saw your banjo. I'm sorry. I won't disturb your things again. I promise you I didn't look at anything else."

James carefully eyed her. Smiling, he took a sip of coffee he had brought from the table with him.

"It's all right, Mrs. Hollister. I don't own anything of value except for that old banjo. And money-wise, it isn't worth anything."

"Do you play?" Caroline said with relief.

"I do. My father taught me. He bought it for me just a few years before he died. That was in '40."

"So you have been playing for a long time?"

James laughed. "I guess you could say that. I was thirteen when my father gave it to me. We used to sit on the porch in the evenings and play together. My mother would rock back and forth with a smile on her face and her eyes closed while we played."

"Your mother must have enjoyed your playing," Caroline replied.

Again James laughed. "Yes, she did. In fact, she used to say that's why she married my father. He was the best banjo player in the county."

Caroline joined in the laughter.

"Did he play any other instruments?" she asked as she stopped laughing.

"I don't think there was an instrument my father couldn't play. He had an ear for playing."

Caroline became somber. She thought of her husband's guitar under the boys' bed.

"Did you…did you take it to war with you?"

James looked at her for a moment and then into the fire. "The banjo? No, I didn't. I'm glad I didn't. It would have been destroyed if I had…or…or someone else would have it today."

Caroline watched as a sober expression crossed James's face as he pulled the banjo from the quilts. He wistfully smiled and fingered it carefully.

"My father said music was the gateway to the soul. It could fill you with joy or melancholy or peace."

"He was right," Caroline answered, her voice low. "Mr. Cartwright, would you play your banjo for a while? I feel I could use a little music right now."

James fingered the banjo again and carefully placed it on his knee.

"Only if you call me James," he answered.

Caroline bowed her head, raised it, and smiled.

"If I call you James, then you can call me Caroline. But," she looked toward the boys, "but only when the boys aren't around."

James nodded and looked toward the boys. 'I understand,' was all he said.

Placing his fingers on the strings, James began to strum and play. The music was slow, rhythmic, and filled the quiet room. Slowly, he began to pluck the strings and tunes began to ring out.

The boys stopped looking at the book and turned to listen to the music. Jumping up, they began to dance around the room.

"This is like at Grampa's," Timmy shouted, "only he plays the fiddle!"

James smiled and began to play a more lively tune. The boys clapped their hands to the music while laughing and twirling each other.

After a few tunes, the boys slowly turned back to the book they were looking at. James began to soften the music and slower music began to come from the strings.

Caroline and James became buried in their own thoughts as James's fingers moved on the strings. Each was in a world that seemed an eternity away.

Caroline remembering the music that once filled her happy home as her husband laughed and she danced around with the children.

James remembering the music of his childhood with his father playing beside him and his mother smiling as she listened to the sweet tunes. And, in recent years, the somber music that was playing in his heart when there was no hope left in him except for a letter.

Chapter 10

Sunbeams crossed the room through the kitchen window. Dust played across the light and onto the floor.

Caroline opened the door and looked out at the puddles of water and mud that were the remains of the melted snow. Birds chirped and fluttered from one fence post to another. The rooster crowing added to the peaceful din that was breaking the silence of the hollow.

Breathing deeply, Caroline closed her eyes and embraced the cool air. Her face burned from the breeze that came through the door, but it felt good.

A lull in winter. A break. A time to relish the peace and tranquility before another possible snowstorm would come through.

Turning around, she bumped into the man standing behind her. Tottering, she leaned forward to keep from falling.

James's arms immediately encircled her.

"I...I'm sorry, I didn't know you were there," Caroline stammered.

"No, it wasn't your fault. I shouldn't have been standing so close behind you," James answered, gazing into her eyes. His arms didn't move. "But, I guess I am glad because I kept you from falling."

Caroline cleared her throat and moved away. Her heart raced. She could feel her face flush. She could feel her throat closing. Breathing deeply, she forced air into her deflated lungs. She had to regain composure.

"Yes, well…well, I…. I'll have breakfast ready shortly," she finally got out. "You…you and the boys will have time to feed the animals."

James lowered his arms and looked at the floor. With a sigh, he looked up again and nodded. His own heart raced.

"Boys! Boys, it's way past time for you to get up. I shouldn't have let you sleep so late. Get up, it's time to feed. There are lots of things that need to be done today. It is beautiful outside and we have work to do," Caroline exclaimed as she moved toward the pan of water on the counter top. Her hands shook as she lowered them into the cool water.

"Caroline –," James began.

"Please, just go with the boys and take care of the animals. I need…I need to fix breakfast."

James looked at her for a moment and then turned to get his coat and hat.

Leaning against the counter, Caroline let out a long sigh as James and the boys left. She could hear their talking as they walked down the dog-run and then down the steps. Quietly, she straightened her hair, smoothed her apron, and continued to prepare breakfast.

James looked around as he walked toward the shed. The heavy snow and high winds had done damage to the building. Wooden shakes were turned up and a few completely missing. A portion of the log fence needed to be reset and braced. A leather strap had come off the door to the corncrib and was dangling.

"Looks like it will be a busy day, boys," he said as they passed a small corral and walked into the shed. "The cow needs to be out for a while. She needs sunshine like everything else. While she's out, I can repair the shed."

Tommy groaned.

"You all right, Tommy?" the man asked as he rubbed the boy on the head.

"I was hopin' we would go huntin' agin today," Tommy answered. "I love to hunt with you!"

"Well, that would be nice, but I have to work for my keep. Your mother isn't going to let me stay here and be lazy. I have to pay my way. That's the right thing to do."

Nodding, Tommy moved to the corncrib and dipped a bucket into the dried corn.

"Just the same, I wish I was huntin'."

"In due time, Tommy, in due time. We get the chores and repair work done then we can hunt. First things first. Work is more important," James replied with a grin.

He knew the boys were sick of being cooped up in the house. The few times they got out they romped and played, trailed the dogs and rabbits, and enjoyed the freedom of the outdoors.

"Mr. Cartwright, do you have any kids?" Timmy asked abruptly.

James was taken aback. It was a simple question, but he hadn't been prepared for it.

"No, no, I don't," he answered, throwing straw into the hens' nests.

"Why not?" Tommy asked, looking in his direction.

"Well, I guess it's because I never got married."

"Would you like to have kids? Kids like us?" Timmy was also staring at James.

James frowned. He tried not to look at the boys. He didn't know what was going through their minds. He wasn't sure what was going through his own mind.

"Well?" Tommy asked, moving closer to the man.

"Well, what?"

"Would you like kids like us?" Timmy asked again.

James stopped and sat down on a stool. Lifting his head, he looked at each boy in turn. Their faces were shiny from the cold. Smears of dirt lay across their cheeks.

"I would very much like to have boys like you. It's every man's dream to have sons who are hard workers and have good character. It just hasn't happened yet. Someday, I hope it will."

"Our maw don't have a husband anymore," Tommy blurted out. "Our paw died in the war. He didn't come home. We're hard workers. We have a good farm."

James looked away.

Were the boys trying to play matchmaker?

Trying to blink back the surprise, James sighed deeply.

"Boys, your mother is a fine woman. She didn't have to let me stay when the weather was so bad, but she did. I appreciate every thing she is doing, but only the good Lord knows what is best for your mother. Come spring, I will be riding out of here so I can find a job. I may even have to go back home in south Arkansas. You have a good life here. Your mother has a comfortable home and you boys to take care of. She is doing all right and she will continue to do all right. The Lord will take care of her. Someday she may find a new husband and you boys will have a new father. It will be at the right time for all of you. Wait and see. Everyone will be happy."

The twins looked at each other and shrugged.

"But, it won't be you," Tommy answered with a glint in the corner of his eye. "I like you. How do you know you're not supposed to be here?"

James was shocked. Then thoughts formed.

How did he know he wasn't supposed to be there?

His heart began to pound. Pressure filled his eyes. His mouth dried. He couldn't swallow.

Was he supposed to be there? Was there a reason, besides his own, for him to be there? It wasn't by accident that he was in their shed. He knew where he was and why he had come there. How could he explain it to anyone? How could he describe his feeling for the place even before he ever came? How did he know it wasn't all God's plan?

Realizing the boys were staring at him, James licked his lips and tried to bring moisture back into his tortured mouth. The pain in his chest wouldn't go away. He had to do something to change the conversation before his emotions - .

"Awe, I'm just a stranger that took refuge in your shed. I needed a place to get out of the weather and your place just happened to be in the right spot. Now, we need to get the chores finished before your mother gets upset because we have been gone so long."

James motioned toward the milk pail and hurried out the door. Laying his head on the wooden fence, he shuttered. He hadn't reckoned on such events happening.

"What have I done?" he whispered, "What am I going to do now?"

Looking at the door of the shed, he hit the fence with his fist. Quickly he moved to the wooden rail fence that was down and repositioned the logs. It wouldn't take long to repair. He would need wooden braces, nails, and a hammer. He could find those in the shed. He just wished the boys would hurry and get the cow milked. He hoped the conversation about Caroline and him was over.

The boys soon were coming out the door. James noticed they came out empty handed.

"Boys, did you forget something?"

The twins looked at each other and shrugged.

"I got the eggs," Timmy said as he held up a basket with one egg.

"Where's the milk?" James asked, cocking his head.

Tommy looked on the ground around him. His eyes grew large as he grabbed his mouth.

James laughed and tussled the boys' hair.

"Boys, go back and get the milk. Someone needs to carry it into the house, don't you think?"

"Yes, sir," Tommy replied as he turned back to the shed. A few minutes later, he returned. Some of the milk sloshed out of the pail as he walked toward the house.

James reached over with a laugh and took the pail.

"I think we might get more into the house if I carry it," he said with a grin.

"We've prayed for Maw to have a husband and us to have a paw," Tommy said flatly as he handed the pail to James. "Are you sure God didn't send you here?"

James didn't want any more conversation about him being there for a divine purpose. He didn't want to talk about him being in the shed or him staying longer than spring.

"You boys are something else," he said as he climbed the steps to the cabin. "I'm afraid what you want probably will not happen."

Not unless Caroline feels the same way I feel, he thought.

Breakfast was quiet. James was afraid to say anything; afraid the boys would bring up the conversation they had outside. But it didn't come up.

As soon as the meal was over, he grabbed his coat and hat.

"There was some damage from the storm. I'll be outside working on the fence and a few other things."

Caroline nodded and continued cleaning off the table. With a break in the weather, she also had work to do. The wash needed to be done.

Hammering braces into the ground, James finished just as the boys were coming out of the shed. They had been cleaning the chicken house and the shed. A wheelbarrow full of manure and hay sat at the door.

"Make sure it's put where we can get to it in the spring," Caroline said from the cabin door. She had the water pail and dipper in her hands.

Watching the boys dump the manure, she handed the water dipper to James.

"That will be good fertilizer on the garden in the spring," she said with a smile.

James nodded and tried to move the fence. It was sturdy.

"Tommy, why don't you let the cow and calf out of the shed? The fence is fixed and they can't wonder off," he said as Tommy ran back toward the waiting adults.

"Yes, sir," Tommy replied as he returned to the shed. Moments later the cow and calf were in the pen.

"Looks like we have a good start for the spring," Caroline said as she started back toward the cabin. "The pen is fixed and we have fertilizer started. I love spring. Everything will start again soon here on the farm. What a wonderful time!"

Spring, James thought, *a time of new beginnings. Would this be the beginning he wanted? Did God have plans of intervention between Caroline and him? Could spring bring love for them or would he move on to find a life somewhere else?*

Chapter 11

The boys were getting louder and louder as they came into the cabin. The morning had been nice and they had worked hard around the farm. If wasn't until they had gone into the shed where James was sharpening the kitchen knives that the arguing had started. They were fighting over a squirrel cap James had made. Caroline was getting exasperated with them as they continued their quarreling inside the cabin.

"Mr. Cartwright said he would make another one," she tried to calmly say. "That one shouldn't be torn apart before he has a chance to finish the other one."

"But, this is from the squirrels I killed!" Tommy yelled. "It belongs to me. Timmy's is the one that he's making."

"These were my squirrels. I saw where he put the skins and they are mine. It belongs to me!"

"Boys!" Caroline screamed. Closing her mouth, she gave a deep sigh, counted to ten, and then started again.

"Boys, bring the cap to me. When the other one is finished I will give this one back."

Hand outstretched, she received the cap and hung it on a peg.

"Now, you two get out your books and read for awhile. You need to keep up your studies. Reading is very important."

"Yes, Maw," the boys answered in unison.

"I'm sorry that I've caused a problem by giving that cap to the boys before I had the second one ready," James said as he got in on the tail end of the heated conversation. Placing the knives on the pie safe, he turned to Caroline. "I'm glad I didn't make a coonskin cap out of that one coon I killed and skinned."

"So am I! Can you imagine what the fight would be like if you had? You've only killed that one coon and it would be chaos around here."

James laughed loudly. Shaking his head, he imagined what would have happened.

"I don't know if the squirrel caps will last long. Maybe I'll get another coon and be able to make two caps before they wear these caps out," James commented as he turned back toward the door. "I'm heading out to the shed now so I can do the last of the work on it. I'll bring the squirrel cap in when I come back. I think I will check on the animals and bring in wood, also. The weather looks better but you never know. I may need to chop up a little more before dark," James said.

Timmy watched the exchange between his mother and James. He wasn't sure what to think of their actions. Caroline smiled and moved with happiness. Happiness that he had not seen in a long time. James spoke quietly but he also had a smile. He didn't act as stiff and weary. He was jovial and made Caroline laugh. Timmy wondered -

Crossing to the door, James grabbed his hat and coat.

"Is there anything you need out of the barn?" he asked.

"You can check to see if there are any eggs," Caroline answered. "I don't think there will be, but you can check. And, if you don't mind, you can milk the cow. That would keep the boys from fighting about who will have to go out into the cold. Oh wait! I forgot, the calf gets the milk in the evenings. How silly of me! I don't know what I was thinking."

The boys giggled and pointed at their mother.

James looked at the boys and then back at Caroline. Nodding, he opened the door and moved into the cloudy afternoon light. A few minutes later the sound of the axe came from outside. Soon it stopped and except for an occasional word being deciphered out loud by Tommy as he read, there were no other sounds.

Finally Timmy turned back to the book he was reading. It didn't take long until he closed it. His reading was fluent and he had finished his story quickly.

"That's pretty lonely work out there," Timmy said, cutting his eyes toward his mother. "Maybe we need to go out there and keep him company."

For a while, he thought his mother didn't hear him. Finally, she seemed to have a reaction.

Caroline turned and looked at the boys. Moving to the tablet she kept for writing, she jotted down several math problems. Handing the tablet to Timmy, she quickly spoke.

"Boys, I think I will walk outside for a few minutes. I don't think Mr. Cartwright has seen the spring yet. Maybe we will walk up there and make sure there are no dead animals around it," Caroline said as she slowly took her shawl off the back of her rocking chair.

"We...."

Timmy hit his brother in the ribs and frowned.

"I think that's a good idea, Maw," he answered still frowning at Tommy. "We don't need dead critters in our drinking water."

"We've already taken him to the spring," Tommy whispered.

Again Timmy hit him in the ribs. Frowning, he gave his brother the shush look.

Caroline opened the door, listened as the axe started again, and then went down the steps toward the sound. It stopped again. She watched as James went into the shed.

Crossing the yard, she stood before the shed. Hesitating, she almost turned around but didn't. Reaching out, she took the handle of the door and pulled.

James heard the door open and turned from the brace he was placing in a corner.

"I thought…I thought you might like to walk up the mountain and check the spring. It might get bad again and we need to make sure there are no animals in the water," she stuttered out.

"I was just finishing up. Give me a second and I'll be happy to walk up there with you."

Turning back to the brace, James used the hammer to get it into place. Slanting the nails, he secured the brace and then pulled on it to see if it would hold.

"That takes care of the shed. I've replaced the shake shingles that came off and braced this corner. It should be as good as new."

"Thank you," Caroline answered as she looked around the room. "Now would you like to go up to the spring?"

"I would like that very much," James replied. Hope filled him.

Caroline held her shawl close as they walked. A light wind had picked up and the air was becoming cooler.

"How bad was the war here?" James asked after crossing the creek and getting into the trees.

"It was bad. The regular soldiers came through and fought whoever was in their path. They took whatever they wanted as they marched toward the south. We were told many people packed what belongings they could and went to Jasper to live in the caves after the soldiers kept coming through. They were afraid of the soldiers and…and the raiders. The raiders went through the hills stealing and killing. There were confederate and union officers who paid them. They laughed about being paid to roust the people and steal from them. They also burned homes and fields. Fear gripped us all every time the dogs barked," Caroline answered, stopping to take a breath. "Thom said the peddler told him raiders were still hitting some areas. The war is over but they seem to get enjoyment out of what they do. They've become robbers, killers, and thieves."

Caroline's eyes swept the forest and looked into the shadows. They hadn't advanced far up the hill that lay across the creek but the woods looked dark and almost forbidding.

Walking in silence for several minutes, Caroline finally stopped and turned around to look below. Looking out, she could see the cabins. She and James were near the rocks she and the boys had taken refuse in a few years earlier.

A shudder went through her body. Her mind jumped back four years.

Caroline had taken the boys for a walk up the hill looking for muscadines. It wasn't long before the dogs started barking. She looked back and noticed there was a commotion toward the cabins. She told the boys to stay behind a large rock while she walked back toward the hollow. As she stood behind a tree, she watched a man gun down Joseph, her brother-in-law. The sounds of the men laughing echoed through the valley and forest. She watched as they turned on the older man with his hands to his head. Thom wasn't given a chance. He was severely beaten and left on the ground a few feet from his son.

She couldn't see Sarah, her mother-in-law. Panic filled her. Her baby was in the cabin where the men were going in and out. Stepping out, she started to run down the hill, but stopped.

What could she do? Waiting until the men were gone, Caroline told the boys not to leave the safety of the rocks. Cautiously, she moved down the hill and into the clearing. Blood covered the ground around Joseph. She knew there was nothing she could do for him. Slowly, she moved past him to Thom. A gash ran across his forehead. Blood gushed from his lips. Leaning down, Caroline felt his chest. He was still alive.

Looking up, she ran to the house and opened the door.

"Sarah! Sarah where are you?" she yelled.

No sound. Caroline quickly ran through the small cabin. She didn't see the woman or child.

Freezing, she stood in the middle of the floor. Fear flooded her. "Sarah!" she screamed.

"Is it safe to come out?" a small voice asked from the kitchen.

Caroline quickly had turned around and saw Sarah's head sticking up through a door in the floor.

"Sarah! Oh, Sarah, are you and Alice all right?" she sobbed out.

"We are fine. Thom had us get in the root cellar when the men came. Are the men gone? Is…are Thom and Joseph all right? Caroline, are they all right? There was so much yelling and laughing. And, then…and then I heard a shot!"

Caroline let the tears slide down her face.

"Caroline?"

"Thom is hurt. We need to get him into the house and take care of his wounds."

"What about Joseph?" the older woman whimpered out as she handed the baby to Caroline. "What about Joseph?"

Caroline's mouth had become dry. She couldn't speak.

Without another word Sarah handed Alice to Caroline and had rushed out the door. Caroline could hear the gasps as Sarah found her son lying in the dirt. The screams reverberated through the valley.

Caroline shook her head. She had to stay in the present. The past hurt too much. Slowly, she focused and stared toward the cabins. There was peace all around in the valley. Smoke was billowing out of the chimneys. The dogs were lazily laying in the yards.

The memories were jarring. She could see every detail of the horrific day. It would be easy to let it fill her with the same dread she felt at that time. It was all too vivid, too surreal. She didn't know if time could ever erase it.

"I…I watched as my brother-in-law was murdered by men that came into the hollow. They beat Thom so bad that we thought he was going to die. It was weeks before he regained consciousness. The men, they…they were…brutal. There was no reason for them to be here. There was no reason for them to do what they did. What they didn't take, they destroyed. They burned the fields…they burned our food supply…they trampled the garden before they burned it! As they left, they torched the houses! I was so afraid. My baby was in that house!" Caroline whimpered. "It was senseless. I'm so glad my boys weren't in the yard. I'm so glad they didn't…. I can't dwell on the past. I can't dwell on the past! The war is over! We have to adjust and move forward."

"Caroline, are you all right?" James asked as he grabbed her arm. "You're shaking like a leaf."

Caroline's eyes bugged. Her lips moved but no sound came forth.

James slowly lowered her to the forest floor and encircled her with his arms.

"It's all right. The war is over. The children are safe. The houses didn't burn. They're still down there. Shhh, honey, it's all right."

"We'll never be safe as long as bushwhackers still come around. Bushwhackers like those men from Missouri and the like!"

Suddenly anger took the place of the fear that had taken hold of Caroline.

Yes, she knew the name of one of the men who came that day. She had heard his name several times as the men laughed and taunted. She would never forget!

"Why are you here?" she bitterly asked into James's shoulder. "Why did you have to come and remind me of the war?"

Pulling away, Caroline pulled her shawl tighter. It was binding her arms and turning them red.

Letting her go, James nodded. His hands shook. He moved them up and down his britches' legs then curled his fingers in and out.

How could he explain? James knew one day he would have to.

Chapter 12

The sun continued to dry the ground. The temperature warmed and the boys stayed outside as much as they could.

Caroline watched from her scrub board and washtub as they carried two big rabbits to their granny.

"I'm glad they wanted to share the rabbits," she said as she dipped another pair of britches into the sudsy water and rubbed them on the board.

"They are good boys," James answered. He had brought out his banjo and was slowly picking the strings as he sat on the steps.

Laying the britches in a basket, she looked over at James. Slowly, she picked up another pair and washed them.

"Why did you come to the mountains?" she suddenly blurted out. "Why didn't you stay in the delta? It's beautiful down there. It's so peaceful."

"May I ask a question before I answer? I would like to know why your husband joined the Confederate army. He joined men that were from the southern part of Arkansas to fight. Why?"

"What business is that of yours?" Caroline squeaked out. Anger still filled her.

James could feel the anger. It heated the woman's face. He had to find a way to calm her.

"I told you I was from the Mississippi delta. My family plantation is there. After seeing the mountains, I can't imagine your husband being down there. Was it because of you? Were you the reason he was fighting for the south? I promise to give you an explanation if you will just tell me why he was fighting for the Confederacy and why he moved you up here. Thom said most of the people up here were northern sympathizers. Why the south?"

Caroline's knees weakened. Air flooded out of her body.

"It's simple, Mr. Cartwright, my family lives in the delta. We lived near Holley Point. My father was in the Arkansas senate. I occasionally accompanied him to Little Rock. Thomas and I met on one of those trips. He came down with a senator from up here. He kept coming down to the farm and then finally went to work with my brothers on a farm that my oldest brother owned. The farm was successful. My other brother soon married and he helped my father with our farm. They all owned plantations and grew cotton. My brothers taught Thomas how to farm using the Negroes."

James cocked his head and straightened.

"So, he moved to southern Arkansas," he said aloud.

"Yes, and after about a year we got married. By then Thomas was a full fledged partner in the cotton plantation and gin my brother owned. Then the war began. When my brothers decided the land was in jeopardy, two of the three joined the confederacy. It was decided my youngest brother would stay on the farm and keep all of them going. Thomas joined the infantry with my brothers."

Caroline raised her chin high. Slowly, she let it drop as she let out a long sigh. "He loved my two brothers that went to war. Only one of my brothers returned."

"But, why would he leave you and the boys here? He didn't have to join the Third. He could have joined one of the Arkansas troops that defended our state. I don't understand why he would bring you here and go down south to join the military."

"Thomas was adventurous. He had ambitions of one day running for the legislature or maybe become governor. That's why he came to Little Rock to begin with. Then he realized most of the voting population lived in the southern part of Arkansas. He thought by joining my brothers in the service of the Confederacy, he would get more recognition," Caroline answered. Slowly her body slumped. She felt tired. She wiped her face with her apron. "You still haven't told me why you came here."

"I came because of...," James stopped for a moment and looked at Caroline. "I came because there was a man from the mountains who talked about his life up here. I didn't personally know him, but I knew of him for a long time. I was with the Third Arkansas Infantry during the war, also. The Third had many regiments of men. All of them went through a lot. We marched to Virginia to join the southern volunteers there. There were many battles. Lots of men were killed during those battles. There were so many skirmishes that I can't recall them all.

"When we got to Virginia, we were under General Robert E. Lee in Northern Virginia. We fought in many skirmishes near creeks and on mountains. We were even mocked by other states' volunteers for our looks and...and the behavior of some of the men. But, we were fighters. Not one of our men gave up. I guess it made us tougher. It didn't matter if we were being eaten by mosquitoes or freezing in the snow, we continued in battle. Casualties fell every time we fought. It was heartbreaking. We left behind good men at Antietam, Fredericksburg, and Gettysburg, along with many other places.

"Some of the companies had to join others because so many were killed. Our numbers were growing smaller. Before Gettysburg, we were assigned to the Texas Brigade. Someone had it in their mind that we belonged with troops from our own area of the country. We stayed part of the Brigade until the war ended."

James got up and walked around in the cold, damp dirt. He was sweating even though it was cold. His eyes narrowed, veiled by the past.

He could see the smoke of the cannons; hear the screams of the dying men, and then the deathly silence of the aftermath. The smell of warm blood filled the air like perfume. The stench of death penetrated the soul.

"You don't know what it was like. You just don't know. Gettysburg was where we were to take a stand. The fight was the worst we had seen. Union soldiers came from everywhere. Fighting was going on all over the place. We could hear the cannons in the distance. We knew they were approaching. We just didn't know how many. There was no turning back. Then the exchange began. Men were falling all around. Your husband...your husband was a brave man when he fell at Gettysburg. They all were. You and all the wives should be very proud of them."

James stopped and ran his hand through his hair. His breathing was heavy. It was hurting his chest. Tears choked him. He had to swallow the lump in his throat.

Caroline gasped, but held her tears. Agony filled her. She could feel the pain inside the man before her. It was devastating; pounding into every corner of the mind, body, and soul.

She had to keep control. She couldn't waiver. There was too much at stake. Did he know more about Thomas? Did he know him but was afraid to say so?

Sitting down on the steps, Caroline wiped her hands on her apron.

"James, would you come over and sit down?" she said as she motioned toward the steps.

Slowly, James lifted his head and looked in her direction. Standing still, he took a deep breath and sniffed.

Again, Caroline motioned to the steps and nodded. Lowering her head she watched him out of the corner of her eye.

James's feet began to move toward where she was sitting. He ran his hand through his hair again. His breathing was jagged.

"Are you all right now?" she asked. He weakly nodded. Taking another breath, she nodded and spoke again.

"Why did you decide to come to the Ozarks?" she asked again. "You're from the delta, why the mountains?" Caroline quietly asked.

"I got restless when we were in the east so I walked around the camp in the evenings. I listened to many stories that were told around the campfires. One group in particular drew my attention. The men in that company were real fighters. They didn't seem to be afraid of anything. They were made up of scouts and rode point. They were fearless yet they had a sensitive side that baffled my mind. One man's tales made me stop and listen. He talked about his home in the mountains of northern Arkansas. He said if you stand on top of a mountain where the trees are sparse you could see forever. The mountains were as blue as midnight on a moonlit night and layered themselves against a bright blue sky. Then, he made you envision them as the sun was going down and they stood blue against a fiery yellow and red sky. He talked about how much he missed the tall stately trees and the beautiful colors of fall. He talked about the hunting and fishing and how good it was. He missed the comforts of home and his family. He wanted to get back to where there was music being played as the evening sun was going down and the tranquility in the soul made one want to just sit back and take in the peace and comfort. He wanted the war to end so he could get back here."

"You still haven't said why you are here," Caroline repeated. Pain gripped her. This man before her was describing how her own husband felt about the mountains.

Shuttering, she raised herself up and breathed in. She didn't want to hear about the war; the war that had taken her precious husband from her and the children.

James stopped and ran his hand over his face. Dampness covered his cheeks. His heart ached. His breathing was labored. His eyes looked into the past and watered. He felt a wave of nausea.

"James? James, are you all right?" Caroline quickly asked. Her own heart was beating fast.

James cleared his throat and let out a sigh. His mouth was dry.

Caroline watched him for a moment. He looked beaten down. His shoulders slumped and his face paled.

"What made you think you could find peace here? Why couldn't you find the peace you were seeking at home in Monticello?" Caroline repeated again soberly.

Her own emotions began to swell. She wasn't sure if she wanted to really know why he was there, yet there was urgency in her own being.

James sensed the change in her and began to gain control. He couldn't let her see him so vulnerable again.

"I had never been to the northern part of Arkansas. I had never seen mountains until the war. I was restless. The war had changed things. I couldn't sit still, so, I decided to get away. I had to make a change. I had seen so much that my soul needed to find peace. I thought about the picture the man had painted of this place; the hours he spent talking about its beauty and the wonderful people who lived here. He made it seem so serene and peaceful. He loved his home and his family. He loved these mountains. I *needed* to feel those same feelings."

Caroline bowed her head and wept. James put his arm around her and patted her hair.

"My husband felt the same way. He called this heaven on earth. But, he wasn't satisfied living here. He had more ambitious dreams. I miss him so much. He was my life. Our sons' life. It isn't the same without him seeing the boys grow and learn new things. He should be teaching them how to chop wood and kill squirrels. He should be here with us!"

"I'm sorry, so sorry that the war had to touch your life and take your husband away. War has touched so many lives. It tore down the family unit by taking

147

loved ones from so many. I wish your husband hadn't been taken from you."

Caroline stared at James for some time. His face was drawn and pale. Finally, she wiped her face and shook her head as she smoothed her apron. She continued to pull little pleats into the fabric as she spoke.

"It's not your fault, James. You were a soldier yourself. You could have been killed as Thomas was."

"Caroline," James whispered, "Caroline, I want to make a difference for you and the boys. I –

His lips brushed her hair. Laying his head on hers, he closed his eyes. Emotions ran through him.

Caroline didn't move away. She moved closer. Warmth filled her.

Finally, he raised his head and pulled his arm from around her. His heart ached. Again a lump formed in his throat. He could hardly breathe. He wanted to kiss her.

Caroline wiped her tears. Looking toward James, her heart surged. Quickly, she lowered her eyes.

What just happened? She thought. *Did I just want to put my arms around him? I must be going crazy. I couldn't have felt my heart go out to this man. It must be my imagination.*

"I...I think I need to go into the house. The...the boys will worry about me being gone so long."

"They are at their grandparents. Caroline –

"Shhh, don't say anything. I...I need to go into the house."

Caroline quickly stood and ascended the steps. She didn't care that the wash wasn't finished. She didn't care that there were wet clothes in the basket that needed to be hung on the line. She had to get away. Get away to the safety of the interior of the cabin.

"Nothing happened," she whispered as she closed the door, "Nothing happened. I imagined it all."

Chapter 13

James stared at the hay strewn ground of the shed. He tried to calm himself. His body quivered. Sitting down on the hay, he ran his hands through his hair.

"What was I thinking?" he questioned himself. "I've never done anything so crazy! What other reaction could I expect? Dumb, dumb, dumb!"

Slowly getting up, he moved toward a shelf in the darkest reaches of the shed. An old blanket was tucked away behind jars and broken tools. Placing his hand on it, he slowly pulled it from its hiding place. He moved his hand from one end to the other. The woolen blanket had been with him for a long time. The color was faded. It was ragged and torn in many places. Carefully, he placed it on his knees and cried into it.

The tears slowly began to cease. Wiping his face on his sleeve, James tried to remove the wet dirt smeared across his cheeks. Unrolling the blanket, he let a tin cup clank to the floor. There were letters tied with string and a small leather pouch. He pulled the worn leather pouch from the blanket. A small rag doll lying on top fell to the ground. The small thud made dust fly for a moment and then settle back down.

Holding his breath and hesitating, James looked toward the closed shed door. No sounds outside. Slowly picking up the doll, he looked at it for several minutes before putting it back into the blanket.

His thoughts returned to the other object in his hand, the worn brown pouch. Breathing heavily he turned the it over in his hands several times. Finally, he opened the pouch and pulled a faded, wrinkled letter from it. Dark stains penetrated the paper and almost obscured parts of the writing.

Dark stains of blood that had been shed years before: blood of the man whom the letter belonged to.

Carefully James opened the delicate pages. His eyes ran over the words. He read them over and over.

My Dear Thomas,

It has been so long since I received your last letter. I was getting very concerned. It thrilled me when your father brought the mail from the peddler and there was a letter from you.

The children and I miss you so much. I hope you are well and will be home soon. Your parents are well, but your father heard there were union soldiers in the area. We are very careful how far we venture from the cabins. Also, we keep vigil so as to know if anyone comes into the hollow. They have gotten more dogs to warn us of intruders.

I miss you my dear husband. The children are growing so fast. The boys miss you. They can't wait until you come home and teach them how to play music. I know they are their father's children and will learn quickly. They also keep sneaking my knife out of the kitchen. I really have to watch them. They so want to carve wood just like you.

Little Alice is toddling now. She walks everywhere and gets into the boys' things. You should see her. She has your eyes and hair. She is going to melt your heart and be the apple of your eye. The boys will have to toe the line and give over to her as she gets older.

I long to hold you in my arms once again and tell you how much I love you. I can't wait for the war to end and for you to come home. I miss the long walks, the singing, the music, and the look in your eyes when you are with our little family. I want to share in your enthusiasm and joy at everything the family does.

I hate the war, but I know you are where you feel you need to be. I support you for fighting for justice and right. I put my trust in the Lord that you will be kept safe and sound and that you will return to us soon. I wait with great anticipation for your next letter.

Remember, you are loved and missed. There are those who await your return with joy in their hearts, warmth in their embraces, and smiles upon their faces. Praying time will pass quickly and you will return home safely.

Your loving wife, Caroline

Pulling the letter toward his chest, James held it as tears came once again. Laying his head over, he wept bitterly until there was nothing left. Raising his head, he straightened the pages and pressed them down. In one motion, he folded the pages and returned them to the pouch. Quietly, he placed everything back into the blanket and rolled it up. Walking back to the dark hiding place, he started to stuff it back behind the jars.

Suddenly, James stopped and buried his face in the blanket. The stench of war lingered throughout the fibers. Blood, sweat, and tears had mixed with the fabric and integrated themselves with the dirtiness of war. Nothing could wash them away. Nothing but death itself.

After a while, he lifted his head, straightened himself, and stared around the shed.

"How can I tell her I love her," he said to the chilling air. "How will I ever be able to tell her the truth. I don't want to hurt her."

Looking toward the loft, James opened his heart to the Lord. He had to have strength and encouragement. He had to have answers about what he needed to do.

"I can't continue," he sobbed. "I know I need to leave before there is anymore pain. I can't hurt her or the boys. I don't want any more hurt for myself. I don't know what to do! Do something, God, do something!"

Pushing his feet around in the dirt and hay, James grimaced and shook his head. Rubbing his face, his chest heaved heavily. He knew what he wanted. He knew when he left Monticello.

"I just want a home, Lord; a home with a wife and family. Take me where I can find happiness and make a family if this isn't the right place for me."

Caroline puttered around the kitchen, trying to stay calm.

"Maw, is Mr. Cartwright coming in soon? It's getting late," Timmy asked.

"Do you want me to go get him?" Tommy chimed in.

"No! No, he will be all right. He's checking on things in the barn, that's all. He'll be in soon."

"What time are we going to Grampa's and Granny's?"

"What? Oh, we'll leave in the morning. I forgot that we are eating dinner with them tomorrow. I'm glad you reminded me it is the Sabbath. I need to leave Mr. Cartwright some food for his noon meal.

"Why can't he go with us to eat?" Timmy asked, sitting down at the table.

"No! No, he doesn't need to go. This...this is our time with your grandparents. This is special for you boys. Now, you boys get ready for bed. It's your bedtime."

Caroline's hand shook as she smoothed her apron.

"Maw, are you all right? It's not our bedtime. We haven't even had supper yet," Tommy exclaimed.

"I'm hungry," Timmy added. "What are we having for supper?"

Caroline looked around the room. For a moment fog surrounded her. Slowly, she began to focus on the wood stove. Stew was on it.

"We...we are having stew," she said as calmly as she could. "We are having stew. It's on the stove."

"Do you want me to get Mr. Cartwright? He needs to eat, too," Tommy asked.

"No, he will come in when he is ready," Caroline sharply answered as she got dishes down for the stew.

Timmy walked over beside her and put his arm around her waist.

"Are you all right, Maw? Do you need some help?"

Caroline laughed and shook her head.

"You are such a sweetheart," she said, kissing him on the head. "I'm…I'm just tired and with it already dark outside, I just forgot what time it is. You go wash your hands. I have everything under control."

Timmy squeezed her waist and turned toward the washpan on the cabinet.

Outside, James washed his face and hands in the cow's trough. The meal was half over when he opened the door and came in.

"I thought you were going to miss supper," Tommy yelled out.

"I…I'll get your plate," Caroline said as she quietly got up.

"I'm not hungry, ma'am," James quickly answered.

"You have to eat. Winter can make you sick quickly if you don't eat and keep your strength up," she answered.

Placing his plate on the table, Caroline sat back down and continued eating. She didn't look at the man standing in front of her. She couldn't. She felt him sitting down more than seeing him.

Biting his lower lip, James sat down quietly and stared at the plate.

"Maw makes the best stew. She used those rabbits you killed yesterday to make it," Timmy said. He kept looking from his mother to James. Puzzled, he tried to make conversation. "Don't you like it?"

James moved his food around in his plate. Looking at Timmy, he nodded.

"Yes, yes, Timmy, it looks very good. Your mother is a good cook. I guess I just got cold outside and I'm just too chilled to eat right now."

"If you don't want it, I'll take it," Tommy quickly said.

"Tommy! No, you will not take J…Mr. Cartwright's food. He needs to eat it. It's a long time to breakfast," Caroline chided.

Slowly, her eyes met James's. There was a long, searching hold. His eyes were red. The lids sagged. There was no light or life in them. There was only darkness, pain, and –

Finally, Caroline lowered her eyes. Anxiety filled hers.

What had happened to the man who had taken shelter in the shed so many weeks earlier?

Chapter 14

Days passed. James didn't say more than a dozen words to Caroline. He would have chores finished before she got up in the mornings and then he would spend most of the day cutting wood, hunting, or piddling in the shed.

"What are you boys and Mr. Cartwright doing in the shed? You spend an awful lot of time in there," Caroline said one morning. "I'm surprised you haven't been trying to snoop around to see what your Christmas presents are."

"We are staying out of your hair," Tommy giggled. "It's been nice outside so we don't want to stay in the house all the time. Can't we do that, Maw?"

"I guess so, but you stay out there so much. Are you sure you aren't up to something?"

Timmy looked at his mother and smiled. His face was smug.

"We might be making something special for your Christmas present. But, you will just have to wait and see. It won't be long now."

"Maw, you know we don't keep secrets from you. We're just having man time, that's all," Tommy chimed in, raising his eyebrows. "Besides, we can't have you a surprise if we have to stay in the house all the time."

"I understand. No, it wouldn't be a surprise if you made me something with you sitting right here with me. So, I guess it is all right," Caroline said with a frown, "Wait, man time? What is 'man time'?"

"You know, we talk about how we are going to help with the planting this spring and what needs to be planted. Sometimes Grampa has Mr. Cartwright helping him sharpen the tools and stuff like that," Timmy answered, shrugging. "That's when we can't work on your present because we want it to be a surprise for Grampa and Granny, too."

Caroline frowned again. She didn't pay attention to the rest of what Timmy was saying. All she heard was that Thom had gotten friendly with James. They would sit and drink coffee or walk around the land as Thom pointed in different directions and made gestures.

She wasn't sure if Thom had plans for James to stay longer than spring but she knew she was going to hold him to the spring deadline for leaving. She didn't need him at the farm any longer than that. There were too many complications arising.

A knock interrupted her thoughts.

Tommy ran to the door and stepped aside as his grandfather came in.

"Thought I'd see if James would like to go down and meet the peddler with me. Do you have anything to send? I'm going over to check on Talbot while I'm out. He was by a couple of days ago and had a bad cough. Sarah is sending some liniment."

Caroline hastened to the cedar chest and pulled out a couple of wool blankets, a few aprons, three scarves, and two shawls.

"I need to see if he will trade for these. I need those items we talked about a couple of months ago."

Her head motioned toward the boys.

"Oh, yes, I remember," Thom replied with a laugh. "I'll for sure check and see what he has."

"I also have a letter to my parents written. Please give it to him so he can post it for me. It has been a while since I posted a letter to them."

"No problem." Thom eyed Caroline for a moment. "I guess you let them know everything is all right here?"

Caroline caught his meaning and looked away.

"I told them the boys have been learning to hunt but I didn't...."

"Grampa, can we go?" Timmy excitedly cut in.

Thom looked away from Caroline and turned to his grandson.

"Not this time, boys," Caroline answered for him. "While they are gone, you boys are going to take a bath. I let you off the hook the last time. You need a bath. You are going to start stinking if you don't."

"But, Maw," Timmy began.

"Don't 'but, Maw,' me, young man," Caroline said with a stern look. It has been over two weeks since you had a bath. I don't want to hear any arguments. Besides, look at Toby. If that dog is going to stay in the house he needs a bath, too! I can smell him from here. You can use your water to bathe him when you are finished."

Tommy laughed and grabbed the dog around the neck.

"He does smell like that dead 'possum he found."

Caroline nodded and winked at Thom.

The boys watched as the two men rode out of sight down the hollow and then turned with scrunched up faces toward the kitchen where the waiting tub was sitting.

After bath water was emptied and all the water had been mopped up from the splashing and shaking by the dog, Caroline settled into her rocking chair to repair and patch some of the boy's pants.

Timmy plopped down on the floor in front of her.

"Maw, do you like Mr. Cartwright?"

"What? What do you mean? I…I – "

"I think he would make a good father, don't you?" Timmy said, picking at the old cloth rug. "I mean me and Tommy like him."

"Timmy, it's not that simple. We don't know that much about Mr. Cartwright. He…he has other plans. In the spring he will be leaving. He's just here because of the weather."

"I think God sent him," Timmy said as he smiled up at his mother.

Caroline blushed as she looked away. Her mind was jumbled and bumfuzzled.

"Timmy, why are you saying such a thing? There isn't anything between Mr. Cartwright and me."

"I like the way it feels with him here," Timmy replied, "He is nice to us and acts the way I think a father should act. Tommy and me have been praying for a father and he might be him."

"Yeah," Tommy added as he sat down beside his brother, "and it's like he belongs here. He makes me feel good inside and he's teaching us so much. He might be the father we asked for."

"Boys, I...I can't believe you are saying such things! Mr. Cartwright is a nice man, but he is only going to be here for a short time. Please, don't get your hopes up. He may not feel the same way."

Caroline wadded the britches up and placed them back into her sewing basket. Her hands shook. Getting up, she hurried out the door.

"Maw, I think he –," Timmy began.

Caroline didn't hear. She had to get away. The boys had shaken her. Breathing heavily, she moved into the dense woods and up the incline of the hill behind the house.

Stopping by a large rock part-way up the hill, she turned and leaned against it. She could see the house from her position.

"What is going on?" she breathed out. "I can't believe the boys were saying such things!"

Closing her eyes, she slowly began to pray.

"Lord, I don't know what to do. This is such a strange situation. I...I do have feelings but I don't know how James feels. I can't let my boys be hurt. I didn't realize how they would react to him being here these last few weeks. I didn't know he would impact them like he has. And, Lord, I didn't know they were praying for a father!"

Sinking down beside the rock, Caroline began to weep.

"Thomas, why did you have to leave us? You were the one I fell in love with! You're the one that was supposed to be here with your children and me! I need you! I need you --."

The sun moved across the sky. Caroline realized she had been away for quite some time. Sighing deeply, she stood up and leaned against the rock to steady her shaky legs.

"Lord, I'm going to take one day at a time. I don't know what James' intentions are. I don't know if it was by accident...or...if it was your will that he was in our shed. All I know is that I must keep my guard up. I mustn't let my boys be hurt but I also must not let them see the turmoil I feel. It's almost Christmas. I want them happy. I must keep a happy face for them."

Slowly, she began to walk back down the mountain. She could see the boys coming out of their grandparent's cabin. Suddenly, she realized they were looking for her. She had never walked off before and left them alone. They were probably panicking.

As she cleared the shed and was almost to the house, the boys ran to meet her.

"I didn't mean to upset you boys. I'm sorry I left the house so abruptly," she said, kissing them on their heads. "I won't do it again."

I'm sorry I upset you, Maw. I won't mention having a paw again. I'm happy just having you," Timmy sobbed.

"Oh, Timmy, you did nothing wrong! Don't ever think you did! I love you so much!" Caroline answered, tears running down her cheeks.

Tommy placed his arms around her.

"We don't need a paw. We can do all the chores and hunting and fishing. Grampa can help us learn the other things we need to do," he said into her chest.

"Shhh, it's all right. Don't worry about it. It's over. Let's go into the house and I'll get you boys some milk and cookies."

Evening brought the men back into the hollow. The horses were draped with cloth bags hanging from the saddlehorns.

Caroline met them in the yard. The boys were finishing the evening jobs but they came running when they heard voices.

"Made a good hall," Thom said from his saddle. "I'm not coming in. I need to get these things to Sarah."

Turning to the boys, he motioned to them.

"I could use your help up at the house. I'm kind of tired after the long day we've had. I could use a hand carrying these in to your granny and putting the horse up."

Running beside the horse, the boys chattered on and on. Soon, they were away from the house.

"Thom was able to get the things you wanted. He even bartered for some store candy. Where do you want the boots?" James politely said. He didn't look Caroline in the eyes.

"I am so glad!" Caroline answered.

Suddenly, she blushed.

He mustn't know about the conversation that went on while he was gone, she thought. *I must act the way I did before. I must stay calm and friendly.*

"Bring them in the cabin, please. I have coffee made. You must be tired and could use a cup."

"I could use a cup," James replied, pulling the bags from his saddle. Looking around, he could see the boys taking the saddle from their grampa's horse.

"I'll put these in the cabin and then I need to unsaddle my horse. Thanks for the coffee. I could stand a cup."

Caroline watched as James carried the bags into the house and then led his horse to the shed. Turning she climbed the steps and vanished into the house. Supper was ready and she needed to put it on the table.

Lord, don't let the boys bring up their idea again. It would be too embarrassing.

Chapter 15

"Boys, I think you just about have your mother's present down perfect. I don't think it could be any better," James told the boys as they sat in the cold shed.

Tommy pulled his gloves back onto his hands.

"I'm glad," he answered quickly. "I think my fingers are almost frozen. I don't think I could stay out here another night. I bet it's almost midnight!"

Timmy shook his head and rolled his eyes. Turning, he spoke to James.

"Mr. Cartwright, I think Maw will love her present! Grampa and Granny will be surprised, too!" Timmy then turned to Tommy and added. "Tommy, our hands will warm up. Don't be so dramatic and complain. What we did is good. You did good."

Tommy nodded and tucked his hands under his thighs.

"I know they will warm up as soon as we get in the cabin. Can we go in now?"

Timmy shook his head and started toward the door.

"Tommy," Timmy called to his brother over his shoulder, "if you want to keep this secret until we go to our grandparents, you have to keep quiet and not give it away."

"I can keep secrets!" Tommy snapped. "You wait and see. I keep secrets as good as you!"

"You better," Timmy warned.

James watched the exchange. He wondered if either boy could keep what they had been doing secret.

Walking into the cabin, Caroline turned and smiled at the threesome.

I have to act normal, she thought, *I can't let any of them think there is anything wrong.*

"Get your hands washed. Supper has been ready for awhile. You took a long time out there feeding. Was everything all right?"

"Fine," the boys chorused. With a giggle, they hurried to the basin and splashed the water as they tried to wash their hands at the same time.

Shaking his head, James tried to force a smile at Caroline. It didn't work well. He found he had to turn his head away.

"They must be mighty hungry," he finally laughed out as he watched water dripping down elbows and onto the floor.

Caroline handed each a rag to dry on and then pointed at the floor. The boys reached down and wiped up the water and then gave the wet rags back to their mother.

The meal was animated and the boys rushed through it with zeal.

"Tommy, tomorrow is Christmas! We need to hang our stockings! I bet I get more in mine than you do. I've been a lot better than you," Timmy exclaimed as he left the table after supper.

"You have not! I'm as good as you! Ain't I, Maw?"

Caroline rolled her eyes.

"Boys, you find the craziest things to argue about. Please, just get your things ready for tomorrow. I guess in the morning you will find out."

Soon the stockings were hanging on the hearth.

"You did put up clean socks, didn't you?"

"Yes, ma'am," they excitedly answered.

Timmy ran to James and sat down in his lap. Putting his mouth to James's ear, he began to whisper.

"I think Tommy's going to keep quiet. It will be the first time if he does."

James laughed, nodded, and hugged the boy.

"Come on, Tommy, it's time to go to bed," Timmy said as he hurried toward their corner of the room.

Tommy started toward the bed then stopped. Turning, he ran back and hugged James.

"Mr. Cartwright, do you need one of my socks to hang on the hearth?" he asked.

"No, thank you anyway," James answered. "I appreciate you asking, but I think I'm a little old for a stocking to be hung. Besides if I had a stocking you might not get as much candy."

"That's right!" Tommy exclaimed, moving away from James.

Caroline watched the exchange. With a deep sigh, she followed the boys, helped them with their quilt and blanket, and then waited to listen to their prayers.

"Maw," Timmy whispered, "why don't you like Mr. Cartwright anymore?"

Caroline was startled by the abrupt question.

"I...I never said I don't like Mr. Cartwright," she whispered back. "What makes you think I don't like him?"

"You don't talk to him much or even look in his direction anymore. Are you mad at him?"

"No, no, I'm not mad at him. I think you boys are letting your imaginations get the best of you. Now, go to sleep. Christmas is tomorrow."

"So, you're not mad at Mr. Cartwright?" Tommy added.

"No," whispered Caroline again. "Don't talk so loud. Mr. Cartwright does not need to hear our conversation."

The boys looked in James's direction. He was sitting in the overstuffed chair near the fireplace. His eyes were closed.

"I think he's asleep," Timmy said as he looked back at his mother. Cocking his head on the pillow, he pursed his lips then spoke again. "If you're not mad at him, why do you not talk to him? I think you need to talk to him. He helped us with your Christmas present and I think you are going to like it."

"Yeah, he's nice, Maw. I think Grampa and Granny are going to like the present, too," Timmy whispered. "We like him. You need to be nice to him."

Caroline's eyes grew wide and then narrowed. Were the boys chastising her?

"I…I think you boys don't understand." Stopping, she looked into their faces. "All right, I will talk more to Mr. Cartwright. I guess he is a nice man. I didn't mean to…never mind, you boys need to go to sleep now. It's getting late and there will be lots of excitement going on tomorrow. I don't want you two grouchy because you didn't get enough rest tonight."

Timmy reached up and hugged his mother again.

"I understand," he whispered. "Mr. Cartwright looks unhappy just like you do. I think you need to pray. I think both of you are afraid."

If you only knew, Timmy, if you only knew, Caroline thought as Timmy laid his head back on his pillow.

"And, I think you are older and wiser than your age," she whispered back, quietly rising from the edge of the bed.

Soon, she could hear even breathing coming from the bed. Quietly, she hurried to her room and brought out a small bag, two wrapped packages, and two blankets.

"I'm glad Thom brought this candy home when he met the peddler a few days ago. I don't know what I would do if he and Sarah didn't help me."

James watched as she pulled the candy sticks from the bag. He wanted to say something, but words wouldn't come. Closing his eyes, he sniffled and gritted his teeth.

Caroline avoided looking at him. She didn't want to get into a conversation. She had to keep her distance, at least until she could calm herself and decide what she needed to do.

The house was finally quiet when Caroline slid under her covers. Cold had crept into the room after she closed the door.

Lying in the dark, she let a tear slide down her face, across her neck, and onto the pillow.

"Lord, how could I betray Thomas like I did? How could I let the touch of another man bring out feelings I shouldn't have? It's wrong, isn't it? I have to send him away, don't I? If not for me, it would be for the boys' sake. They are getting too attached to him. But, how can I send him into the cold? How can I go back on my word that he can stay until spring?"

Caroline stopped and readjusted her pillow. Again, she pulled her hands beneath her chin and spoke into the air.

"How can I keep from having these feelings if he stays? How can I avoid them? Lord, I have to put it all in your hands. I can't do it, but you can. Strengthen me and give me peace that none of this will happen again."

Turning over, she tried to sleep. It wouldn't come. The sound of wind against the window didn't bother her. It was her heart.

James sat in front of the fireplace. He watched the flames dance around. Crackles came from the blocks of wood. A spark occasionally sizzled up the chimney.

Running his hands through his hair, he slumped in the chair.

"Lord," he silently said, "I need help. Just looking at Caroline makes me want to pull her into my arms. I know I can't. I don't think she feels the same way. And, what about the boys? Lord, I am so attached to them. I love those two. Should I leave before I get more attached? I don't want to put pressure on the boys or on Caroline. I can't see them hurt. They have been through enough."

As morning broke, James was still in the chair staring into the almost dying embers. Slowly he got up and stoked the fire and added more wood.

Looking at the stockings, he reached into his pocket and pulled out two small knives. He slowly put them into the stockings.

Christmas Day had always been special at home for him. His parents' home was alive with music, food, and family. When they died, he was left with one brother and two sisters. They had families of their own. They stopped meeting as a large family and had Christmas on their own.

His fiancé had made plans to do the same.

His fiancé. The woman he had planned to spend the rest of his life with; the woman who was to bear his children; the woman who married his best friend a month after he left with the Third.

Shaking the thoughts off, James moved back to the chair he had spent the night in.

"That's all in the past," he said to himself. "It's been over for a long time. I'm not going down that road. It doesn't do any good to have self-pity."

Looking around the warm room, James sighed.

"I wish there could be a new beginning here," he continued. "I want what is here."

"Did you say something?" Caroline asked from her bedroom door.

It startled James.

"No, no, I was just talking to myself. It's nothing. Sorry if I woke you up."

"You didn't. The thought of the boys waking up did."

James smiled and nodded.

Soon the house would be lively as the boys bounced around looking at presents. Caroline would be watching with love in her eyes.

Chapter 16

"Maw, this is the best Christmas ever!" Tommy yelled. "I love apples!"

"The gloves and socks are so warm! Now, my hands and feet won't get so cold when I go outside. And, I can't believe you kept new boots a secret! They just fit! Thank you, Maw!" Timmy added.

James waited. The knives must have slid down to the bottom of the socks with the candy.

Suddenly, Tommy jumped up and started dancing.

"Maw, a knife! A real knife! How did Santa know I wanted one!" he exclaimed.

Caroline sat up. Her eyes widened. Looking at James, she started to say something but stopped.

He was nodding at her. Turning back to the boys, he spoke softly.

"Mountain boys need to know how to use idle time for profit instead of wasting it."

"Their...their father used to say that," Caroline stuttered out.

"All the carved animals you see around the room were whittled by him," Timmy said. Getting up, he grabbed a deer. "This one is my favorite. I remember him telling me that some day he would teach me how to do work like this."

A tear breached the corner of the boy's eye. Quickly, he brushed it aside.

"I would like to learn to whittle. I may never get as good as Paw, but I can try."

Caroline turned to the side to keep the boys from seeing her tears. She remembered the long cold evenings when Thomas sat by the fire and carved out copies of the animals that roamed the woods around them. He would pick up the shavings before bedtime and smile at her.

"*'Mustn't leave a mess for my beautiful wife, he would say.'* During the summer, he whittled outside. Company kids were always taking something home with them when they visited. There were at least twenty or thirty of his whittled animals somewhere in the mountains where children played with them."

Clearing her throat, Caroline got up and busied herself in the kitchen.

"We are having leftover biscuits with butter and jelly for breakfast. You need to have time to get the chores done before we leave for your grandparents'."

James approached her cautiously. Standing just behind her, he shuffled his feet.

Turning around, Caroline almost fell into his arms. Straightening, she looked into his clear brown speckled eyes. Her stomach churned.

"Boys, start the chores and I'll be out to help you in just a few minutes. The quicker we finish the quicker you can head toward your grandparents' cabin," James said over his shoulders.

The boys clambered into their coats, boots, and gloves. They hurried out the door and were yelling all the way to the barn.

James' eyes never left Caroline.

Caroline started toward the hearth. Reaching it, she took a brown paper bag down.

"I almost forgot, I have a present for you," she said.

James looked at it. His heart sank. He didn't know if he should take the present. What he had to say would change things.

Clearing his throat, he looked at the ceiling then spoke. "I plan to leave when you do this morning. I'll tell the boys goodbye after I help them get things taken over to their grandparents place. I don't want to be a burden on you or on them."

Caroline was stung. She couldn't believe what she was hearing. An ache filled her.

"James, I…," she started, "I don't want you to leave. Not yet. It would spoil the boys' Christmas if you left today. My in-laws are expecting you to be with us when we go over to their cabin. I wouldn't want to hurt Thom's feelings. He's such a good man."

"Caroline, you know how I feel. I don't want to put you through anything that would hurt you. If I stay much longer, I wouldn't be able to leave the boys. I love them."

"You can leave after Christmas. I don't want the boys Christmas to be spoiled!" she cried out, turning her back to him. "Please, just stay until after Christmas."

James continued looking at her. It took all the power he had to keep from reaching out and turning her around. He wanted to hold her, kiss her, and tell her how much he loved her. But, he couldn't. He stood there with his heart in his throat.

"All right, I'll go help the twins and then I'll help everyone get ready. I'm not hungry. I'll send the boys in to eat and when you are ready to leave, I'll be in the shed waiting. Just have one of them come and get me."

Slowly, he moved to the door, got his coat, and went out.

Caroline leaned against the cabinet. All strength left her. Closing her eyes, she breathed deeply. Her body trembled, hands shook.

Lord, why didn't I let him leave? It would solve everything! Do I really want him to stay for the boys? Or, is it for me?

The twins shattered the silence in the room as they came in stamping their feet.

"It's snowing again!" Timmy excitedly said from the open door.

"We're going to have a white Christmas!" Timmy exclaimed behind him.

Caroline gathered herself together and took the warmed biscuits from the stove. She hurriedly put the butter and jelly on the table along with a knife and spoon.

"My favorite jelly!" Tommy said, "I love muscadine jelly!"

"There's nothing you don't like," Timmy threw back. "You'd eat a dead 'possum old Toby brought up if Ma would cook it."

"I do like 'possum, but I don't want one that stinks and the dog has been chewing on."

"Boys, we don't have time for you to go through all the things Tommy likes to eat. We need to get breakfast over and then get things ready to leave," Caroline interjected.

"Maw, can't Timmy and me run up to Grampa's? We could get there before you ever leave the house," Tommy asked as he picked up a picked up a biscuit.

"No, you can't. We will all go together. Now eat, boys, we have to go."

"Isn't Mr. Cartwright going to eat with us?" Timmy asked.

"No, Timmy, he isn't. He said he would be in the shed until we get ready to go."

"Oh," was his reply.

"I know why he stayed in the shed," Tommy spoke up. "He wants –

"Tommy, hush!" Timmy said. "Don't say anything else. We don't want to spoil the surprise!"

"What surprise?" Caroline asked as she looked from one boy to the other. "What are you up to?"

"You'll see," Tommy answered with a grin. "Granny and Grampa will be so surprised just like you. I can't wait to see your faces!"

"Don't say anything else, Tommy! Please!" Timmy pleaded.

"Okay, okay, I won't," came the reply with a snicker.

Stepping outside, Caroline was surprised to see the hitched wagon near the door.

"It started snowing, so I thought it might be better if we took the wagon," James said as he picked up one of the boys and put him in the back of the wagon. "It might get worse before we decide to come back here."

"The cabin isn't that far away," Caroline answered. Quickly, she bit her tongue. "I suppose it is better to be prepared. It will be easier to take everything up to the house in the wagon than it would be to try to carry it in the snow."

James made sure the boys were carefully wrapped in the quilts in the back of the wagon. He winked at the boys and padded the lump beside them. The boys giggled and winked back.

Turning, he walked to the side of the wagon and climbed into the seat next to Caroline. He looked at her to make sure she also had wrapped herself in a quilt.

The snow was coming down hard as the foursome pulled away from the house. Soon, even the tracks they left behind would be covered and only a wonderland of white would be there.

"Maw, old Toby is following us," Timmy said from the rear of the wagon.

"Honey, he knows where he is going. He is all right. He goes up there all the time. Don't worry about him," Caroline answered.

The older Hollisters only lived a short distance away, but the going was rough with rocks everywhere. The road was narrow; almost a wide trail. Snow was beginning to bank on the trees and rocks. An occasional hawk could be heard.

James thought he saw a glimpse of other wagon tracks along the way but wasn't sure. He carefully fingered his shotgun that was leaned against the seat.

Smoke was coming from the cabin in the foggy hollow as they moved through the now heavy snowfall. James could hear dogs barking as they drew closer to the weathered building.

He could see why the Hollisters had settled in the little valley between the two mountains miles from the nearest settlement. It was peaceful and quiet. There was plenty of game to kill and a nice, flat garden area. A creek ran through the property near the house; a creek with deep holes where summer fishing took place.

Pulling up, he tied the horse to a fence post. Another wagon was nearby. Helping Caroline down, he caught a glimpse of Thom approaching from the house.

"I'll help take things in," he said as he reached the wagon. "This weather is getting nasty. You may have to spend the night."

"Spend the night?" Caroline laughed. "We live right there. It's walking distance. We will not have to spend the night."

Toby jumped around near the wagon and sniffed the dogs that were now circling the wagon. Soon, they were all running toward the back of the house.

"I see Bob and his family or Margaret and her family are already here," Caroline said, picking up a bag.

"That's Margaret and her bunch. They got here about an hour or so ago. Bob came in last night. He didn't stay long. He said the family is sick and Jane didn't want to get the kids out," Thom answered. "It will only be those that are here celebrating with us. But, I am still blessed to have all of you here."

"I feel blessed, too, Thom," Caroline answered. Hugging his neck, she smiled at the older man. He was thin and had sadness in his eyes. She knew he had wanted Bob and his family to be there but it didn't work out. They had missed many Christmases during the war and now sickness was keeping them away.

Chapter 17

James was the last to enter the warm, cozy dwelling. The smell of food filled the air. A mixture of savory and sweet greeted him. His stomach growled.

"I'll put these quilts over in the corner," he said as he carefully put down his load.

The quilts seemed oddly draped and bulky in James's arms. Caroline decided in the rush to get out of the snow they were just thrown haphazardly into his arms.

The twins snickered and then covered their mouths.

"What's going on," Sarah Hollister asked.

"Nothing," Timmy replied with raised eyebrows. Again, he snickered.

"Mama, I want you to meet James Cartwright," Thom said as he led his wife of forty years to where James was standing. "It has been a blessing to know the family is being taken care of during this bad winter."

"I've heard so many nice things about you, young man. You are so welcome to be here to celebrate with us. It's so hard to be away from family and friends at a time like this. It must have been a bitter and sad time for you when you couldn't be with them. I hope we can make up for part of that."

Caroline stared at her mother-in-law. She couldn't believe what she was hearing.

"This here is our daughter, Margaret, and her husband, Stephen. Those two scalawags over there are Jason and Hardy. The little one Margaret is holding is Lilly," Thom continued with introductions.

Margaret nodded at James while Stephen shook his hand. The two little boys didn't pay him any mind. The oldest was about the twins' age and the other about a year younger. They were busy talking to their cousins about what they had gotten for Christmas.

Sarah stepped up to Margaret and tickled the baby. Smiling, she looked around the room.

"Well, it's nice to have family together for Christmas. I wish Bob and his family could be here but I understand. It's not like we haven't had Christmas without them before, but they will be missed," Sarah said as she wiped her hands on her apron. Looking up at James, she gave him a wide smile. "If my boys can't be here I'm glad to have Stephen and you here."

James felt completely at ease. Thomas' family had welcomed him as a friend. Taking Sarah's hand, he smiled and nodded at her.

"I'm thankful that I can be here, Mrs. Hollister. The invite was most welcome to me. I really didn't expect it."

"Well, you just make yourself at home and visit with Grampa," Sarah answered. Turning to Caroline, she motioned toward the kitchen. "Caroline and I are going to finish up in the kitchen. I still have some cooking to do. Come along, Caroline, we can visit in the kitchen. Margaret, you just take care of that young'n of yours. You've helped a lot and there's plenty more help here now."

Caroline followed Sarah to the table. She saw the food she had brought was still wrapped in towels. Slowly she began to unwrap each one and place it back on the table.

"I brought the sweet potatoes and turnip greens like you asked," she told Sarah, "and, I brought two pies."

"Oh good," Sarah replied. "We can put the sweet potatoes on the back of the stove and reheat them. I'll heat the turnips just before we eat."

Caroline looked over at the men. They were laughing and talking. She couldn't believe how welcome her in-laws had made James feel. If they only knew the turmoil he caused her, she knew they would send him packing.

She kept looking back toward the men as they talked. Occasionally one of the boys would run over to them, all would laugh, and then the men would start talking with each other again.

"It's so nice to have someone to help you and the boys take care of the chores," Sarah was saying.

"What? Oh, oh, yes it is. I try so hard but I can't get enough wood up sometimes. I do appreciate the help."

"He seems like a nice man. What do you think about him?" Margaret almost whispered in her ear. "He is a looker, isn't he?"

Caroline could feel her heart beat faster. Her breathing became labored.

"It's hard to find a good man these days. I know you and the boys can take care of yourselves but it must be hard on the three of you. I guess it is easier if you have a man around. How do you feel about that?" Sarah said as she stirred food on the stove.

Caroline stood staring. Her head ached and her stomach became queasy.

"Caroline, are you all right?" Sarah asked.

"I think the ride over here has just gotten to me. It was so cold in the wagon. I…I just need to sit down for a moment."

Why would her mother-in-law ask such a question? Was she afraid she would develop feelings for the stranger? Was she worried that her son's wife and children would be taken away from them?

Caroline slowly moved to a chair by the table and sat down. She felt numb. Her head began to throb.

"If you're going to sit down, you can hold Lilly while I help Mama," Margaret said.

Caroline could feel the baby being put in her arms but her mind wasn't focused on the action. Her mother-in-law's words kept going through her.

"Maw, Granny said it will be a while before it will be time to eat. We want to show you our surprise! Will you come and sit down in the front room? Please!" Tommy said as he pulled on her arm.

"All right, Tommy, you don't have to be so aggressive. I'm holding Lilly."

"Sorry, Maw, but we are so excited!" Timmy exclaimed as he took his grandmother's arm.

Caroline handed the baby to her mother and followed the other women into the front room and sat down. She watched as James crossed the room with the boys and began to unwrap the quilts he had brought in. Soon, a banjo was in Timmy's hands.

"We've been learning how to play out in the shed. Mr. Cartwright has shown us how to play," Timmy said with a bow.

"It was hard to hide from Maw. Mr. Cartwright had to keep sneaking his banjo out of the house and then back in so she wouldn't see it was missing."

"And, that must be the reason you kept borrowing my fiddle! I thought you were playing it for Caroline and the boys."

"He didn't play the fiddle for us," Caroline blurted out.

"No, he just played for us," Tommy said with a grin.

Everyone laughed and nodded at James.

"Is this the reason you wanted to bring the wagon?" Caroline asked with wide eyes.

"It was going to be mighty hard to walk and sneak the banjo up here," James answered.

"Yeah, we couldn't walk with you and carry it. You would guess what the surprise was!" Tommy shouted.

"You don't have to shout," Timmy exclaimed. "We are all in the same room!" Turning to his grandfather, he added. "Grampa, I need to borrow your fiddle. I decided I could learn the guitar later. I wanted t learn the fiddle so I can play like you. I know you can teach me so much more after…after -- "

Thom beamed and stuck out his chest. "Well, I'm mighty pleased you want to play the fiddle like me! I bet you get better than me in no time!"

Laughter filled the room again but soon ceased. Steven motioned for his boys to sit on the floor at his feet. Music began to fill the air. Caroline's mouth opened and then closed. Tears welled. Her body swayed to the sounds coming from the instruments in her sons' hands. An occasional squeak came out but it didn't matter. They were following in their father's and grandfather's footsteps. The boys had clearly inherited their ability to make music. Their little feet and heads moved to the sounds coming out of the instruments.

She looked over at Sarah. Tears were in her eyes. Her lips trembled.

"If you boys don't mind, I'm going to get my paw's fiddle and play along with you. James, I have a guitar over there if you know how to play it. We'd be happy for you to join us," Thom said as he jumped up and took an old fiddle from the wall. "Stephen, you got your guitar?"

"I sure do!" Stephen answered as he quickly reached for a blanket near the bags brought in from his wagon.

James retrieved the guitar from behind a bedroom door and the music was on. Old Dan Tucker and Turkey in the Straw began to fill the room. Other tunes followed. Peace filled the air. Tranquility entered the soul. Calm made smiles cross the lips.

Caroline watched James as he strummed the guitar. His smile was contagious as his fingers moved across the strings. His toes tapped to the rhythm. His head slightly nodded to the time.

After a short time, the twins put down their instruments. Their fingers were hurting and they had played themselves out. Tommy handed the banjo to James and turned to his audience and bowed. Sitting down on the floor, the boys watched and listened to the men play Jimmy Cracked Corn, O Susannah, and the Old Gray Goose and then change to Christmas and church hymns. Their bodies swayed back and forth to the rhythm of the songs.

"This is so wonderful," Sarah said with a wide grin. "Now all we need is for Margaret to join in. It would make it all complete."

Everyone looked at Margaret.

"Oh no," she answered. "I love hearing Stephen play. Besides, I have the baby to take care of. Maybe some other time I'll play."

Thom turned to his daughter and nodded. "I'm going to hold you to that. When harvest comes in next fall I want all of us to sit on the porch and play. The boys will know more songs by then and we can have a hoedown. We'll get Bob and his family over here and cook up some vittles and have a high ole time."

"Well then, I have so enjoyed every minute of this," Sarah finally said. "It reminds me so much of Christmas before the war. It has filled my heart with the joy of Christmas again. But, I think all of us are ready for some food. Caroline and I will set the table while all of you men wash your hands and get ready to eat. Margaret, I see the baby is asleep. You can put her on the bed. I left the door open so's the room would be warm."

Caroline followed her mother-in-law into the kitchen and got out plates, glasses, and silverware. Sarah began to take food from the stove and put it on the table.

"Mrs. Hollister, let me help you with those heavy things," James said as he entered the area. "I can set the ham wherever you want it."

"It needs slicing first, young man. Would you do the honor and cut it for me? And then you can put it in the center of the table."

Caroline watched as James sliced the meat and placed it on the table. She smiled as he turned to look at her. He took the sweet potatoes from her and placed them next to the ham.

"Thank you," she said softly.

"My mother taught us to help. She would be turning over in her grave if she thought I was sitting back and not doing my share."

"I can't believe she would ever do that. You seem so well mannered," Sarah said, placing golden slices of bread on each end of the table. "She must have been an extraordinary woman."

"She was," James replied, "She was. She made sure we were clean, that we went to school, said our prayers, and read our bibles. But on the other hand, she was playful and full of mischievous love. She kept my father on his toes."

Caroline listened to the banter between Sarah and James. Images of James and his family danced across her mind. She could see them running and playing, yet calm and refined.

"After she passed, my brother and sisters started having Christmas with their in-laws or at home with just their children," James continued. "I went a couple of times to visit but it wasn't the same. Soon after, the war started. I was in the field and not celebrating."

Caroline's heart lurched. A pain went through her. She couldn't imagine being alone during Christmas. She started to speak, but Sarah beat her to it.

"Well, we don't want you alone this Christmas. You are welcome to sit at our table and celebrate with us. The good Lord wouldn't want anyone to miss out on his day."

"Mama, this table looks delicious," Thom said as he herded four hungry boys to the table. "I bet these four are going to eat us out of house and home today."

"Now, Grampa, you stop that. You know I fixed enough food to feed an army. The boys can eat all they want," Sarah said as she patted their heads.

James was sandwiched in between Thom and Timmy. Tommy complained that he should be sitting next to James, so James exchanged chairs with Timmy. With satisfaction complete, everyone bowed their heads for Thom to bless the bounty.

"Lord, thank you for coming to the world so that we could be reconnected to the father. Bless those that have returned home now that the war is over. Help them to adjust to the way their lives will be now that they are back in familiar places. Bless this family and our guest as we feast on the food you have provided for us. Amen."

Noise filled the room as soon as the prayer was over. Tommy was digging into the sweet potatoes. Timmy held his plate and waited for ham to be placed on it.

James looked around the table. Joy filled the room. Everyone was enjoying the festivities. Looking at Caroline, he watched as she interacted with the others.

This is a real family, he thought. *A family with lots of love and compassion. The way my family used to be.*

His stomach drew up. He tried to calm his sudden jitters. His mind raced. He knew what he had to do. He had to be honest with the woman across from him.

How is Caroline going to feel when I tell her the truth? How will she react? Will she hate me or forgive me?

"Can I cut my meat with my new knife, Maw?" Tommy asked. "I can wash it when we are through eating."

"You have a knife?" Thom asked. "Let me see that knife."

Tommy pulled his knife from his pocket and handed it to his grandfather. Thom looked it over and whistled.

"That's a fine looking knife. I know you're going to get lots of use out of it."

"Put it back in your pocket, Tommy. That's not the kind of knife we use at the table. I can see there will have to be rules imposed about those knives. We'll discuss it when we get home."

"Yes, Maw," Tommy answered as he pushed the knife back into his pocket.

Caroline looked at James when she finished her sentence. Putting down her fork, she wiped her mouth and picked up her glass of water.

"Now, Caroline, all boys need a knife. Thomas was eight when he got his first one. We used to sit out on that porch and whittle together. He got better and better. It wasn't long before he could outdo me with every stroke. You let those boys learn how to use those knives. They will learn to respect them after they have a few nicks in their thumbs," Thom replied.

"I loved watching my boys whittle," Sarah added. "Maybe one of them will get as good as their paw was. You never can tell."

Caroline shifted nervously. She hadn't expected her in-laws to be so receptive to the knives. She felt they should side with her. The boys were young. They didn't need a knife.

"I loved the music you boys made today," Sarah said, trying to fill the silence that followed Thom's rebuke. "I didn't know you boys had it in you. You're going to be just like your father. He could play almost any instrument he put his mind to. He was really good, too. Oh, I loved to hear him play just like I did all my kids."

"I wish I could remember him more," Timmy said with his head down. Pulling it up, he smiled. "But, I have Mr. Cartwright to teach me more. He can play real good, too."

"Yes, he can," Thom agreed. "And, you are mighty lucky that he can play the fiddle and banjo. He can help you a lot."

James felt sick. His throat choked. He wanted to get up and run out the door but he was rooted to the chair. Looking at Caroline, he sighed and then sniffled.

I have to tell her when we get back to the house, he decided. *She has to know the truth. I can't be here on pretense any longer.*

Chapter 18

A full moon lightened the sky as the wagon left the cabin. Dark shadows filled the woods on both sides of the narrow road. The occasional sparkle of eyes greeted them as the horse clopped along on the snow.

There was silence in the wagon. The boys were wrapped in blankets and asleep. Toby lay on top of the boys and added a little extra warmth.

Caroline looked at the sharp shadows. The night was peaceful. An occasional hoot would break the silence and then the flap of wings would follow. The crunch of the snow under the hooves of the horse was music that filled the air with the assistance of snow falling from limbs on the trees and the whoosh of wheels crossing the ice and snow.

"We never had snow like this in Monticello," James said, breaking the silence. "I've never seen anything so breathtaking."

"I know. Thomas was with us the first winter we were here. We lived with his parents for a few days. Sarah would watch the kids while we took walks in the snow. He would point out the tracks and talk about what animal made them and which direction they were going.

It was magical. There would be times when we would walk up on a deer or elk. One time, we watched a bear cross the creek and go under the roots of a tree. Thomas said it was late for the bear to be out. That something must have disturbed it."

"Sounds like he made you feel right at home."

Caroline smiled into the moonlight.

"He did."

Silence again filled the air.

Clearing his throat, James whipped the reins and the horse moved a little faster.

"Where do Bob and his family live?"

Caroline looked up and pointed toward the hill on the right.

"They live in the next holler."

"Okay, what is a 'holler'? James asked. "I heard that word earlier."

Caroline laughed and looked back at the boys.

"Haven't you noticed the language up here is a little different? I wouldn't say they speak exactly like we do."

"I have noticed, but it's nice. There are a few words I don't understand, but that's all right."

"Well, holler must be one of them," Caroline said. "It means hollow. It's the little valley between the hills and mountains. Up here they have hills and hollers."

James laughed and nodded. "I understand now."

James helped Caroline from the wagon when they got back to the cabin.

"I'll bring the boys in," he quietly said as he moved to the back of the wagon.

The snow was still coming down but it was lighter. Caroline made her way to the door of the cabin and turned the knob.

Holding the door, she waited for James to bring the first of the sleeping boys in. Quickly, she turned their quilt aside and motioned for him to put the boy down.

James made two more trips to the wagon before moving it to the lean-to at the end of the shed. Taking the harness off the horse, he walked it into the shed and rubbed him down. Giving the horse a little grain and hay, he closed the door and moved through the snow back to the wagon to finish getting everything out. As he brought the last of the quilts and other items in, Caroline quickly closed the door behind him. Walking across the room, she smiled at him.

"I almost forgot, you didn't open your present this morning," she said as she picked it up from her rocking chair.

"I...I didn't get you anything," James responded.

"You did! You gave me a great present. You have spent time with my boys, taught them how to hunt safely, and showed them how to play music. What you did for them, you did for me."

"Caroline," James huskily said, "you are the most giving person I have ever met. You care about everyone more than you care for yourself."

"That's the kind of person the lord wants us to be," she answered with a smile. "Now here, this is yours."

James reached out and took the brown paper wrapped package. Untying the string around it, he pulled the paper open. Inside was a pair of gloves, a scarf, and a pair of socks.

"Very nice," he said, clearing his throat.

"I hope they fit. I wasn't sure what size to make, so I guessed."

"They are perfect. Thank you. No one has been this nice to me in a long time."

Caroline looked around the room and tried to think of something to say.

"Thank you for getting everything out of the wagon and bringing it in. I think I'm going to bed now.

I'm very tired. Good night, James, and merry Christmas."

"Caroline, can we talk?"

"No, not tonight, It has been a long day. I am going to bed. You know where your covers are," Caroline answered over her shoulder.

Stopping at the bedroom door, she turned around and faced James.

"Thank you for giving my in-laws a good Christmas. The boys enjoyed it, too."

"I didn't do anything special."

"Yes, you did! You taught Tommy and Timmy how to play the instruments. That was very special. And, when you and Thom played together I know that made his day."

"I'm glad they enjoyed it. But, what about you, Caroline? Did you enjoy the day?" James waited. He hoped she had forgiven him for not being honest with her.

Suddenly the sick feeling returned to the pit of his stomach. He was still being dishonest with her. There was more he needed to say. She needed the whole truth.

Caroline stretched her arms up over her head and yawned. She didn't answer his questions. Instead, she turned toward her room, entered, and closed the door.

James stood in front of the hearth staring at the door.

Caroline leaned against the inside of the door. Her eyes stung. She wanted to open the door and run into James's arms and tell him how special he had made her Christmas. But, her feet wouldn't move.

With a deep sigh, she willed her feet to take her to the bed. Without removing her dress, she slipped under the quilts and pulled them over her.

Lord, why is this happening? The boys and I have been doing just fine! We don't need anyone else in our lives. We have Thom and Sarah and...and Thomas's brother, sister, and their families. We have all we need! Don't we?

Breaking dawn came through the window. James watched as daylight brightened the snow. Sparkles began to spring up on the frost.

Lord, I ask you again, was I wrong to come here? James rubbed his neck and shook his head. *You don't have to answer that, I know I was crazy. I don't know why I did such a thing! I wish I could take it back, but I know it's too late. Lord, I was so stupid to think....*

Slowly, he pulled his boots on and laced them. Crossing the floor he stoked the fire then turned toward the door.

The air burned his chest as he threw hay to the horse and cow. He didn't see the chickens but he knew they were in the chicken coop where it was warm. Grabbing a handful of corn, he strewed it on the floor. He knew the hens would be up soon and be hungry.

Looking to make sure the water wasn't frozen; James hit it with the axe. Ice and water flew into the air and splattered. Slinging his arm, he tried to get as much water off his arm as possible.

The blocks of wood were frozen to each other when he reached into the woodpile. Taking his foot, James kicked the pile and broke pieces loose. Picking them up, he headed toward the door.

Caroline heard the noise outside. Slowly, she put on her dress and opened her door to the front room. She noticed James was not in the room. Walking to the door, she peeked out. She could see him picking up firewood. She watched as he came toward the door. Hurriedly, she opened the door for him and then closed it when he was clear.

"We have enough in the house for today," James said as he placed the wood into the wood box. "This will dry out as we use the rest. The animals are fed and have water."

"Thank you," Caroline answered as she moved toward the cooking area. There was leftover bread on the cabinet. Unwrapping it from the towel it was in she placed it on the back of the stove to warm. Hurriedly, she put oats into water she had boiling.

"Breakfast will be ready in about twenty minutes," Caroline said, glancing at him. "I'll let the boys sleep in. They had an exhausting day yesterday. Thank you for doing their chores."

"They didn't need to get out. New snow has fallen. There's ice on top of it. Really slick and cold outside. No one needs to be out in this kind of weather."

Caroline nodded and pulled the biscuits from the back of the stove. Oats filled a pot on the front burner. Jelly and butter sat in the middle of the table. A small container of brown sugar was also there.

James stared at the food but didn't move from the hearth.

Using a rag, Caroline lifted the hot pot off the burner and placed it on the table.

"The food is on the table. You need to eat. I'll pour your coffee," Caroline said as she took a rag and lifted the coffeepot.

"Caroline, I need to talk to you. I...I need to tell you something," James started.

Caroline looked into James's face. She couldn't read his expression.

"You need to eat while the oats are hot. Come on, sit down, and eat. We can talk later."

James shifted his weight and then moved toward the table. Pulling the chair out he sat down and bowed his head.

Caroline took it that he was ready to say the prayer and quickly sat down beside him. Extending her hand, she smiled.

"It's nice to have a man in the house who likes to pray. I miss Thomas saying grace."

James flinched, but said nothing.

"I'm ready when you are," Caroline said as she lowered her head.

James stared at her for a long time. Finally, he reached across the table and took the extended hand that had been offered from across the table.

He could feel a knot in his throat as he tried to push the words out. Swallowing hard, he started again. This time with true meaning.

"Lord, thank you for this family. They have been so good to me. There is no way I could ever repay them but I know you can multiply their bounty and bless them with peace, joy, and happiness. And, Lord, thank you for the food that has been prepared by the loving hands of Caroline. Amen."

Caroline looked across the table. She didn't immediately take her hand from his.

Chapter 19

Caroline studied James's profile as she mended a shirt. He was pale and thin. His hands shook as he held his coffee cup. He didn't say much and it seemed hard for him to look someone in the eye.

Had he always been that way or did the war change him? Would Thomas have been the same way if he had come home from the war?

"James, may I ask you something?" Caroline asked as she sat and finished mending the shirt.

The boys were asleep and the house was quiet. Only the crackling of the wood in the fireplace could be heard.

James put his coffee cup down and looked in her direction. Nodding, he cocked his head and waited.

"What was it like back east? I mean, well, how was it during the war?"

James looked back at the fire and then at the cup in his hand. The small amount of coffee jiggled.

"Why do you ask?"

"I…I've thought about what it was like for Thomas. He wrote that it was terrible but he didn't go into detail. I think he didn't want his parents and me to worry. What was it like to be in the army?"

"The war is in the past. Talking about it won't change anything. Sometimes it's best to leave it alone."

Caroline studied him for a moment. Putting the shirt beside the rocking chair, she wet her lips. Picking up another shirt, that needed a button, she sniffed and cleared her throat.

"I want to know. I want to know what Thomas went through. I need to know."

James cut his eyes toward her and then back down to the floor.

"We were in the infantry. There was constant marching. Sometimes we marched for days, snatching a little sleep from time to time, while waiting for scouts to return with news about the road up ahead. Other times we would be hunkered down while storms beat us with wind and rain. Our feet stayed wet. When our socks dried, they would be stiff in our boots and cut into the blisters and soft spots making them bleed.

"We were always on guard watching for...," James broke off and took in a breath, "for our own kinsman to start shooting at us. We didn't know who would be the next to fall. There was no rest, not real rest anyway. Only bloody thoughts going through our heads that were disguised as sleep."

Caroline stared at him. Her heart raced. She could picture Thomas living through it all.

It must have been horrifying, she thought, *simply horrifying. Thomas must have been as affected as James by the turmoil, killing, and pain.*

Shaking her head, she tried to work on the shirt she was sewing. She couldn't. She was too entranced with James' portrayal of what he saw.

"What about the weather? How did you cope with the weather? And, food? Did you have plenty of food?"

James felt a chill run through his blood. His veins popped out on his arms as he doubled his hands into fists. His neck stiffened as his muscles constricted.

"It was miserable. We were constantly moving. There were times we marched for days. The men were so weary and tired we could hardly put one foot in front of the other. Some became so weak that we had to hold them up to keep them from being left behind. We went through mud after rainstorms that swallowed our boots. We could hear the suction as we pulled them up to freedom. Some rivers were so swift we had to help hold the wagons to keep them from being swept away. Some men didn't make it. They were swept downstream never to be found. The regiment didn't have time to look for them. We had to keep moving. Oh, a small detachment was left to look for them and bury them, but we never heard anything more about whether they were found or not.

"During the winter, cold didn't just creep into our clothes and make us cold. It was there all the time freezing our hands, feet, faces, and bodies. In the summer and winter, we were ever on the move and sweat poured from us. During the summer, it would become sticky. The odor of little hygiene was always with us. In winter, the sweat would freeze on our bodies. Our socks would stick to our feet. Frostbite became common.

"Days, weeks, and months passed. There was no escape. We were soldiers. It was our duty to be there."

James stopped and looked at Caroline. Horror filled her face. Her eyes were wide and her mouth slightly open.

"Are you sure you want me to continue?" he hoarsely asked.

Nodding, Caroline blinked. She realized the grip she had on the arms of her chair was making her hands hurt. Loosening her grip, she tried to sit back and relax. She couldn't.

James turned back to the fire and stared into it. He wanted to stop, but found comfort in being able to tell what had happened. There was a release, a calming peace that came over him. He could feel his muscles relax, his heart slow.

"And, then there were the bugs. Ants and spiders crawled on us as we took what rest we could. Mosquitoes ate us alive as we marched through the swamps. Bull gnats attacked us with fierce revenge for being in their territory."

James shifted in his chair. His mind raced back. He could feel every torturing moment he had been in the field. He could feel the anxiety returning. He tried to suppress it, but couldn't. Putting his head down, he puffed out air. Finally, he lifted his head.

"Some bugs we were happy to see. At times, our rations ran low. The Yankee soldiers would cut off our supply wagons. We ate what we could. We would find...we would find grubs and wiggly red worms to eat. There were also beetles and other bugs. They would be a welcome sight to have them when we were hungry. There were times when some of the boys would feel along the edges of the river banks as we walked and snatch up a catfish or some other kind of fish. When we stopped, there would be a quick fire started and the fish would be cooked and hurriedly devoured. Other times we would come up on a farmhouse. There would be corn in the fields, eggs and chickens in the coop, and our captain would commandeer them and we would feast. "

James got up and carried his cup to the kitchen. Putting it on the table, he returned and put his hand on the back of his chair.

"I never thought about that until just now. We ate the food the people grew for themselves. We ate their chickens and eggs. We took from them just as the soldiers took from my farm. It was the same. The men were hungry and they had to be fed. The only difference is that we didn't burn their crops! We didn't, but they did!"

James realized he was pounding the back of the chair. Hitting it slowly one last time, he put his hands to his head.

"I'm…I'm sorry."

Quickly, he turned toward his coat and grabbed it. Opening the back door, he hurried out into the cold, dark night. He had to release the visions that were buried deep inside.

Hurrying to the shed, he buried his face in his hands.

"God, help me! I want to forget the war! I hate what it has done to me! I want peace. Please, *please*, help me."

"James?" a soft voice came from the shed door. "James, do you mind if I come in?"

Wiping his face on his coat sleeve, James tried to calm himself.

"I'm sorry that I brought up the memories of the war. Please forgive me," Caroline apologetically said. "I...I just wanted to know how Thomas must have felt. Again, I am so sorry."

"It's not your fault, Caroline. The war is always with me. I can't get away from it. Every time I think about it, I cringe. I used to not be so sensitive. The war took...took.... I must learn to get over the effects. When I'm with the boys, I can forget for a while. When I...I'm with you or Thom, I don't think about it. I have a new life. It's a new beginning I want. I'm trying to leave it all behind. I'm tired of every time I close my eyes I see the face of some soldier who didn't make it. I'm tired of being afraid and alert every time I hear a noise. I want my life back. I want it to be normal. You...you're helping me do that."

James took a deep breath and looked at Caroline. "Thank you for being patient with me."

You are what Thomas said you were. You are patient, kind, gentle, and loving. You are a beautiful woman inside and out. You let the lord lead you in every thing you do. You are who I dreamed you were all those years I was imprisoned. You are the woman I want in my life; the woman who can take my pain away. Why can't I tell you that?

James's heart was full. He could feel his pulse racing. He wanted to say more….he wanted to say '*I love you, Caroline*'.

Chapter 20

Caroline watched as the sun came up earlier each morning and set a little later each day. Winter was moving forward but was holding on with a fearful fist. There had been few days without ice or snow. Trees crackled and fell night and day. The woods thundered with the noise.

She was glad James and the boys had put plenty of meat on the table. Besides the bacon and ham from the hog Thom had butchered, there were rabbits, squirrels, and coons to eat.

During days of sunshine many chores had to be accomplished. Repairs had to be made and laundry could be hung on the lines instead of inside the house.

The animals basked in the sun and enjoyed being where they could move around and not be closed in. The dogs in the hollow ran, barked, and played.

Caroline smiled as she watched the boys on one of those sunny days. Both loved being outdoors. They found new freedom in being able to run and play without her constant watchful eye.

Rabbits bounded across the yard and skittered in a zigzag as the boys and dogs chased after them. The chickens were no match for them as they grabbed them and threw them into the air. The yard and house rang with the clamor of their running feet and yelps of excitement as they ran through one end of the dog-run and out the other. Their antics were wearisome. They were full of energy; never quiet and still.

Caroline stopped hanging a towel on the line and watched for awhile. Her heart, for the first time in a long time, was full. There was peace and contentment. The boys were being boys. The weather didn't bother them. They were laughing, running, and working with each other.

They loved the outdoors and were anxious to help James with hunting or cutting wood. Even work wasn't a chore.

Caroline smiled as she watched the boys help repair the chicken house after a fat 'possum had gotten into it and killed a hen. She bit her lip when they came back to the yard muddy and laughing when they chased the calf to put it back in the pen with its mother.

"This is the way it is supposed to be," she whispered as she turned back to the wash. "James is good for them. He's patient, gives advice, and smiles at the boys' accomplishments. They rally round him and excitedly work beside him. Their friendship is growing as they share their whittling and continue the music each night."

But, what about when he leaves? Kept nagging in the back of her mind.

"I'm not going to think about it," she said aloud. "I'll worry about that in the spring when he leaves."

Caroline smiled as she finished hanging the last pair of britches on the line. Picking up the basket she started toward the cabin. Looking at the firewood, she changed directions and picked up a log from the pile. A small sprig of green welcomed her.

"Grass," she whispered. "Winter is ending!"

Putting the wood into her basket, she headed back toward the kitchen. She wanted to bake a pie and needed the extra wood in the stove.

Stopping, she turned back to the woodpile. Quickly she rolled a log over the grass. Looking around she smiled. No one was watching.

She sang as she entered the door.

"I didn't know you could sing, Maw," Tommy exclaimed. He was grabbing a piece of bread from the table.

Caroline was startled.

"Was I singing? I didn't realize," she said, putting the wood into the box next to the stove. Her hair was half out of the bun she had put it up in. Her shawl was full of dried leaves. Reaching up, she pulled her hair down and ran her fingers through it. She left it hanging across her shoulders and down her back.

Caroline smiled as she turned around. *Was I singing?* She thought as she patted Tommy on the head. She pulled her shawl away from her shoulders and moved it toward the woodbox. Shaking the shawl she watched as the leaves fell into the box. Carefully she picked off those that didn't fall off.

"Maw, how did Mr. Cartwright know our names when he came here?" he asked as he set up the checkerboard.

"Wh…what did you say?" Caroline stammered. "He knew your names?"

"Yeah, when we went to the shed that first day, he asked if this was the Hollister place. Then, he asked which one of us was Tommy and which one was Timmy."

Caroline was stung.

He knew their names? How could he know their names? He said he was on his way to Mountain Home. Who was he?

"Tommy, stay in the house. Don't argue and don't follow me. I will be back in just a little while."

Caroline hurried into her shawl and rushed through the door. Thoughts ran rampant through her.

Seeing Timmy walking toward her, she motioned for him to come near.

"Go in the cabin with your brother. Play checkers and stay in there. I want to talk to James for a few minutes," she sharply said.

Timmy stared at her but didn't say anything. He knew the tone she used and he had to hurry to get inside.

Standing in front of James, she placed her hands on her hips. Her eyes were wide and her mouth was drawn.

James noticed the anger immediately. His mouth went dry. Trying to swallow, he found there was nothing to swallow.

"Just who are you, James Cartwright? Don't tell me you didn't know what place you were on. Tommy just told me you did."

James looked at her and searched her face. He knew he had to answer truthfully. Slumping onto the stool, he put his head into his hands.

"I was hoping the boys had forgotten," he quietly answered.

"They didn't forget, so who are you? I want the truth, Mr. Cartwright! How did you know you were on our place? We are way up in the holler. We aren't easy to find."

James ran his hand through his hair again. His breathing was jagged.

"Yes, I knew this was the Hollister place, Caroline. I can explain. It will take a little time, but I can explain," James said as he slouched more onto the stool. "I told you the truth about when we camped. There were nights I got restless when our regiment was in the east so I walked around the camp in the evenings. Your husband was in one of the groups that told stories about their homes. I sat and listened as he told stories of the mountains and the mountain people. He talked about playing music and having hoedowns. He said…he said he wished he had never left the mountains and the people he loved. He talked to the men every night. Men from different regiments came and sat with him. They listened intently. They talked about their wives and children. They hated that they had to leave them and hoped the war would not affect them. But, he was the one that talked the most."

"I thought…I thought you didn't know Thomas."

Suddenly Caroline stopped. If he had seen Thomas then he had to have seen her brothers. Her heart palpitated. Were they the ones that talked about their families? She wanted to change the direction of the conversation toward her brothers, but changed her mind.

She had to stay focused. She could ask about her brothers later.

"You just said you listened to him tell about the mountains. You still haven't said how you knew this was the Hollister farm."

James wanted to tell her everything. He wanted to tell her she was the reason he was able to live in a prison camp after he was wounded. Instead, his heart sank. He had to tell her all the truth but his tongue wouldn't form the words he wanted to say. He remained silent.

"How could you deceive us! How could you do such a thing to my sons! You have some explaining to do!"

"It isn't like you think, Caroline. Just…just give me a few minutes and I can explain."

Caroline stared at James. Slowly she took in a deep breath.

"I have been waiting and listening. I will wait a little longer, Mr. Cartwright," she calmly answered. "I will wait, but you better tell me the truth!"

James winced at her words. He was no longer James. She had reverted to calling him mister.

"I said I walked around the encampment. Your husband was in one of the groups of men around a campfire that I walked by. I've already told you the truth about that. I never stopped and visited with him or the others. I would sit outside the fire ring and listen. That's all there was to it at that time. I just listened. Your husband was so passionate about his love for the mountains that it drew me in. He made them sound like a paradise," James began. "I felt the same about where I lived. He made me homesick for my farm and for my family. But things changed when I got home. There was nothing left of my paradise. My home had been ransacked, the fields destroyed. My brothers were home and starting their lives over with their wives and children. They didn't have time for me. I couldn't think. I couldn't handle what I had gone through and then go back to being normal. I had to get away."

James paused and took a deep breath. "I remembered what the man had said about the serenity the mountains had. It filled me with an obsession to see this place for myself. As I traveled north, I looked for the peace. After a while, I realized I was in the area he came from. I found out where the hollow was from the peddler that goes through every few weeks. One thing led to another and I ended up in the shed after it started to snow."

Tears formed in Caroline's eyes. She tried to blink them away. She pictured her own home back along the bayou. She tried to see it destroyed with no fields of green. She couldn't. But, she could see the pain in his eyes. She could see he was seeing it all over again.

"I'm sorry, Caroline. I will get my things together and leave. I don't want to cause anymore confusion or problems. I love the boys."

James looked around the shed. His throat was tightening. His body had grown weary.

"You can tell them whatever you want. I don't blame you for hating me if you do. I was wrong for coming here."

Caroline closed her eyes and shook her head. Her chest heaved.

This man had to leave. He had come into their world and disrupted their lives. He couldn't stay. Could he? No, no, no! He had to leave and the sooner the better!

Caroline wanted to run from the room. Pressure built in her chest. Pain seized her. She looked in James's direction and air escaped.

His head hung low. He looked old and down. The life seemed to leave his body.

Compassion filled her. What was the alternative?

How could she tell this man she didn't want him to leave? How could she explain that the boys needed him? That they loved him and wouldn't understand his abrupt departure?

Closing her eyes, she opened them again and looked at the ceiling. "Right now, Mister Cartwright, I feel confused. There's just so much for me to think about. I...I need to do a lot of praying. I don't know what I think any more. I...I...do know one thing. You can't leave this way, Mr. Cartwright. The boys wouldn't understand if you don't tell them goodbye. We...we agreed you would stay until spring. That isn't very far off. They will understand you leaving then better than you leaving now. When you leave, I don't want you to ever think about coming back."

Chapter 21

The smells of spring exploded into the morning air. The temperatures were changing. The cold didn't bite through the clothes or hang onto the fingertips. Peace was settling into the mountains and forest. More songbirds were returning. The woods were filling with different songs each morning and night. Frogs let their presence be known with their nightly serenades near the creek. Noisy Cicada and locusts drummed out their unbridled buzz that filled the air. Life had awakened in the valley.

Caroline sat on the steps of the cabin and looked toward the eastern sky. Rays from the rising sun were showing just above the mountain. The pink and dark blue sky was giving way to yellow and a lighter blue. Light was filling the little valley.

There would be a transformation taking place in a few weeks. Grass would begin to grow. Various shades of green would fill the woods and brown tree trunks would disappear into the lushness of the leaves. White flowers would be seen peeking out through the other colors along the hillsides.

Soon it would be time to plow and prepare for planting. The fertilizer the boys had been piling up would be strewn over the fresh ground and new life would begin again across the ground.

"You're deep in thought," James said behind her. "I didn't realize you were up."

"I couldn't sleep."

"I'll go back in and not disturb you," James answered.

Caroline half turned and moved over a little. "You don't have to go back in. It…it's all right. You can sit out here if you would like."

"Well, it looks like a good morning to sit out here and enjoy the scenery," James replied sitting down next to her. "It's so calm. I can feel the peace. It fills me with…."

James stopped and looked at Caroline. Her hair was down. It framed her face and made her look young and innocent. The sunrays made her skin glow in the early morning light. There appeared to be a halo around her as she sat and looked out over the land.

He shuddered and realized he wanted to reach out and touch the glowing face. He wanted to caress the hair and hold it in his hand. But he didn't.

"Spring is in the air. I can smell it. I won't be staying much longer. I want you to know how much I have enjoyed being here. It's a time I won't forget."

Nodding, Caroline didn't answer. Her mouth wouldn't form words.

Getting up, James returned to the kitchen and poured a cup of coffee. Looking out the window, he calmed the desire that was alive in him. He couldn't do what he had wanted to do. He couldn't pull her to him and kiss her.

This isn't working, he thought with a sniff. Looking in Caroline's direction, he saw her head drop. He knew she was still angry with him. He hoped she could understand his reasoning and know he didn't mean to hurt anyone.

Caroline took one last look around the hollow. She was still angry with James but it was subsiding quickly. She had listened to him and tried to understand his reasoning but still she was confused.

Lord, give me strength. Help me to let him go. Help the boys be able to handle his leaving. Don't let them be hurt. Give them understanding.

Pulling herself from the warm rays of the rising sun, she returned to the kitchen. The boys would be awake soon and she had to get breakfast ready for them.

Looking around the room she was surprised James wasn't there. His coat was missing from the nail. She knew he had gone through the dog-run instead of entering the house.

Sitting down at the table, she ran her hand through her hair. Thoughts were tangling themselves in her mind. It had been days since she really carried on a conversation with the man living in her home. They had polite encounters but that was all.

As each day passed, Caroline knew she was getting farther away from her encounter with James. It didn't matter as much. He would be leaving in a few weeks and she could go back to her normal life.

"My normal life," she mumbled, "What kind of life is that?"

Putting her head in her hands, she closed her eyes and bit her lips.

"But, he lied to me," she said into her hands. "He might not have known Thomas but he had seen him. He also had seen my brothers! He came here under false pretenses. He has to leave. He doesn't need to be here. It will hurt the boys if he stays much longer."

Raising her head, she looked toward their bed.

I've got to prepare them. He's going to leave and they have to be prepared for that. I mustn't let them be hurt. I've got to protect them.

Timmy began to stir. Caroline watched as he stretched.

"Got to get breakfast," she said aloud. "Those hungry stomachs will have to be fed."

Grabbing a pot, she began to pour water into it. Stirring the coal under the burner, she added more wood and then placed the pot on top of the metal plate she had replaced.

"Maw, where's Mr. Cartwright?" Timmy asked as he came to the table. "He didn't go hunting without us, did he?"

Caroline quickly looked toward the corner where James kept his rifle. It was there.

"No, no, he didn't go hunting. He must be out in the shed feeding the animals. He'll be in soon."

James sat in the shed with Caroline's letter in his hand.

"How could I have been so stupid," he said, hanging his head. "How could I have thought I could come here and everything would be the way I dreamed it would be? It has all been in my imagination. I never should have come. I never should have come!"

Shaking his head, he looked around the shed. Soon, leaves would be coming out on the trees. They were already getting the red tint on the limbs that showed sap was running through them. Flowers would be blooming and grass would cover the ground.

Thom would be getting the plow out and start working the ground. Early crops would need to be planted. The older man might expect him to help.

"I want to do that," James muttered. "I want to help with the plowing. I've never been behind the plow myself, but I know I could do it. I want to help the old man. I want to do something I can be proud of."

Suddenly, the twins' faces came to him. His heart plummeted.

"It wouldn't be fair to the boys," he quietly said. "They deserve better. I haven't been honest with them. They could hate me, like Caroline does, after they find out the truth. I can't let that happen."

Getting up, he picked up the milk pail and moved toward the cabin. As he stepped inside, Tommy looked at him.

"I was wondering where you were," he said, mouth full of oats.

"I was milking the cow," James answered slowly. "You boys were sleeping so well, I didn't want to awaken you."

"Your breakfast is on the table," Caroline told James just as a knock was at the door.

Timmy ran to the door and opened it. Thom stood in front of him.

"Mornin', Timmy, how are you this fine mornin'?"

"I am fine, Grampa," the boy answered with a hug. Running back to the table he picked up his spoon once again.

"Mornin' Caroline, I come by to see if James will help me with the plowin' this mornin'. Sarah said I need some help. She don't think I'm as young as I used to be," he grunted.

Caroline handed him a cup of coffee and smiled. Patting him on the shoulder, she shook her head.

"I was just going to ask why you were out so early. Now, I don't have to. I'm glad you listened to Sarah."

James turned to Thom and nodded.

"What about it, James, will you help me this mornin'? I would be much obliged. I guess Sarah is right, I don't get around like I used to."

James looked at the table. He had planned to make an excuse about leaving and be gone by noon. Now, he was faced with a dilemma.

Thom seemed to read his mind.

"It might be a week or more afore my boy can come over and help. He has his own place to take care of. I know you plan to leave soon, but I could use a hand for awhile. Like I said, I would be much obliged if you would help. It seems this piece of ground gits bigger ever year and it takes me longer to get it worked up. I guess that's because I ain't as young as I used to be." Thom rugged his neck and moved it side to side. "What do you say? Can I count on your help?"

James sat and looked at the table for a minute. Taking a sip of coffee, he looked up at Caroline. She had her back to him. He didn't know what her expression was.

Caroline stared at the dishpan on the cabinet. Closing her eyes, she waited for James to answer. The weather was good. He could leave any day. She was ready for him to saddle his horse and ride away.

"I don't mind helping you, Thom. Everyone needs help every now and then. Besides, working would help pay for my keep while I've been here. I'm just finishing up breakfast. Be with you in just a moment."

James looked back at the table and wiped his mouth on his napkin. Slowly he drank the last of the coffee and pushed his chair back.

"I'm ready," he said as he stood next to the older man. Shaking hands, they turned to the door and started outside. James turned toward Caroline again and tipped his hat. "Mrs. Hollister, that was a mighty good breakfast. Thank you for preparing it."

Caroline turned toward the men and stared as they walked out the door and closed it.

"What...what just happened?" she said, wide-eyed. "Why couldn't he just have said he had to leave? What am I going to do now?"

Chapter 22

Timmy and Tommy stared at each other. Grabbing their spoons, they hurried through their oats and then threw the spoons into their bowls.

"Boys, don't break the bowls," Caroline scolded.

"Grampa might let me plow!" Tommy yelled, jumping from his chair.

"Whoa," Caroline told him. "You are not going out there and pester the men. I don't think your grampa is ready for any help from you. I want you boys to stay out of their way. Do you hear me? Stay out of their way."

Tommy frowned and sighed. "Yes, ma'am," he answered.

"We'll finish the chores and watch from the porch," Timmy answered with a sigh of his own.

Caroline was curious how the men were doing out in the hollow. She moved to the dog-run and peeked around the corner and down toward the creek. She could see James and Thom as they marked off plots and started to loosely plow the top of the ground. It seemed that each year the soil grew large rocks that had not been there the year before. She could see James carry large rocks to the edge of the stream and drop them on the ground.

"I was hoping he would leave," she whispered under her breath. "I need him to leave. Lord, how am I going to handle being around him for a few more weeks? I…I don't know if I can do this. Lord, this is for sure one time you have to give me strength and willpower."

Looking down, she saw the boys were also watching the men. Their hands twitched and their bodies constantly moved. Looking up, she noticed the sun was almost overhead.

"Boys,' she called, "take water to your grampa and Mr. Cartwright. They need to take a break."

Timmy ran to fetch the water and the two boys met up and walked to the end of a row. Standing still they waited for the team to pull the plow to the end of the row. Handing the water to their grampa, they pointed and talked.

"They are talking their ears off," Caroline said to herself. "Those poor men."

As the sun was reaching the top of the sky, Caroline made a cold meal for everyone.

"Tommy," she called from the steps as she descended. "Go get Granny and tell her I made dinner. She can sit out here with us and visit."

Tommy ran to the other house and a few minutes later the older woman and boy came out the door. The woman was carrying a covered plate in her hands.

"I didn't know what you fixed," she said to Caroline as she drew near, "but I brought some teacakes out that I made this morning. I hope the fellas like them."

"If'n they don't I will eat them," Tommy yelped. "I love teacakes!"

"Teacakes?" Timmy asked with a shout. "Granny makes the best teacakes in the world! Can I eat one while we are waiting for Grampa and Mr. Cartwright?"

"No, you may not!" Caroline replied, touching the end of Timmy's nose. "You know better than ask such a question. Now, scoot and go get the men. They need to eat. It's been quite a while since they have had anything to fill their bellies."

"Yes, ma'am," Timmy said as he turned and ran toward the field.

As the men joined the little group on the quilt, Caroline tried to smile. She was glad the conversation was lively between the men, the boys, and Sarah. She didn't feel she could add much to it.

An hour later the men got up and walked back to the waiting horse and plow. Sarah brushed her hair back into her bonnet and helped clean up the picnic area.

"I don't know what to do with these two teacakes that are left," she said, raising an eyebrow and looking toward the boys. "I guess I could let the dogs eat them."

"Granny! Granny, you can't let the dogs eat good food! If'n you don't want them, Timmy and me will take them off your hands," Tommy grunted out. "We don't mind finishing them up for you."

Laughing, Sarah handed the teacakes to the boys. "I thought you might say that. Now, why don't you walk me back to the cabin? I might have a little milk to go with that last teacake."

Caroline smiled as she watched the boys talk to Sarah as they escorted her back to her cabin. Nodding, she decided this would be the daily routine until the ground was plowed. She knew once that was done, she and Sarah would have to be in the fields with the men planting. They would be very tired at the end of each day. Looking up, she decided this might be the year the boys would work beside the men getting the main crops planted while she and Sarah planted the gardens.

"It's time," she decided, "it's time. They have to grow up sometime. Their grampa needs them, so I will tell them just before the planting starts."

Looking up, she saw James coming toward her. His clothes were wet. She knew the men had finished for the day and he had bathed in the creek. Rising from the step she started to turn away.

James caught her gently by the arm.

"I'm sorry," he said. "I know it is hard for you to be friendly with me each day. I'm not doing this to hurt you. I truly want to help Thom with the land. I can move out to the woods if you would like me out of your house."

Caroline quickly turned around and stared at him.

"I can't let you do that! That…that is just crazy! What in the world would Thom and…and the boys think if you just up and went out to the woods?"

"I could say that I'm tired of being cooped up inside and I want to sleep outside so I can see the stars at night."

Caroline half laughed. Shaking her head, she looked at the ground.

"Mr. Cartwright, that would never do. The boys would grab their bed things and move out there with you. No, that would not work at all." Sarah stopped for a moment and then continued. "I have no plans to not be nice to you. My father-in-law needs your help. As long as you are helping him you will stay in the house."

"Thank you, Mrs. Hollister," James answered. Slowly, he walked toward the shed.

Caroline hurried into the house to make coffee.

Caroline sat on the porch and watched each evening as Thom slowly trudged toward his cabin. The boys held his hands and walked with him across plowed ground and up the trail. Sarah would be waiting at the bottom of the steps and help him climb the three steps onto the porch. Having him sit down in a chair, she handed him a wet cloth to wipe his face and hands. She knew he was tired but she didn't know what else she could do.

Caroline was glad James was there to help. He would stay later in the field and continue the work. He walked behind the horse holding onto the plow and breaking more of the clods of dirt as he went over and over the ground. Dark finally drove him inside, but not before he took a dip in the creek.

"Ain't that water cold?" Tommy asked.

"Don't you wade in the water and look for fish? Is it cold when you are out there?" James asked.

"It sure is! I don't want to take a bath in the crick! I'd freeze if'n I had to do that. Why do you take a bath out there?"

"Can't bring the land inside with me," James answered.

"But, you come up here soakin' wet," Timmy said with a frown. "Then you change in the shed."

"I do that so my clothes will dry. I don't want to go into your mother's house with wet clothes."

Tommy twisted his head and looked at James. "But, you have on wet clothes if it's raining. You come in the house then."

James laughed. "Yes, I do, but those clothes are never as wet as these. It's not the same. Believe me, it's not the same. Think about when you go swimming in the summer. Aren't you more wet than when you get wet in the rain?"

The twins looked at each other and nodded.

"Yep, that makes sense," Timmy answered.

Tommy shrugged and smiled. "Wet is wet to me. It don't matter how wet I git."

The boys laughed and then running they climbed the steps and headed down the dog-run.

"Maw has supper ready. When you get changed we can eat." Timmy said as he opened the door.

Light streamed out of the cabin. James could see Caroline through the window. She was in the kitchen putting plates on the table. Turning, James hurried to the shed. He was cold. Standing and talking to the boys had made the water soak into his skin. He needed to change before he caught a cold.

By morning, James's wet clothes were dry and he put them on again for another day of work.

On the fourth day Caroline noticed they were getting worn in many places. Holes were showing along the cuffs and on the tail of the shirt. One knee of the britches was almost threadbare. Looking through the cedar chest at the end of the bed, she pulled out a pair of britches and a flannel shirt. Holding them close, she almost put them back into the chest. With a sigh, she finally stood and brought them into the big room. Handing them to James, she tried to smile as he took them from her.

"They were my husband's," she almost whispered. "I think he would be glad if they got some good use."

Nodding, James laid them over on his bag. "I'll wear them in the evenings after work. The clothes I have on now will be fine to work in when the others are too ragged. I appreciate you helping me. I can really use the shirt and pants."

Stepping outside, James walked to the outhouse behind the cabin. After a few minutes, he returned to the chair he usually sat in. It didn't take long for him to be sound asleep.

Caroline watched him for several minutes. His breathing became even and a light snore filled her ears. Quietly, Caroline picked up one of the quilts and spread it over him. Standing behind the chair, she watched his breathing for a while longer. Reaching out, she almost stroked his hair.

God, how could you let the boys and me have such a good time with this man and then let such bad moments happen? It isn't fair to Tommy and Timmy. They are going to be heartbroken when he leaves. I...I will miss him, too. The time is passing so quickly. He will be leaving as soon as the planting is over. That will be in just a few short weeks.

Chapter 23

James shook the boys early on the fifth morning. Daylight showed through the window and birds were already chirping.

"Boys, your mother has breakfast ready and we have a surprise for you today. Get up and eat and then I will tell you about the surprise," James said as he shook the boys again.

Climbing out of bed, it didn't take long for the boys to have their clothes on and to be sitting at the table. Eggs, bread, butter, and jelly waited for them.

"This is my favorite breakfast," Timmy exclaimed. "What a great way to start the day!"

Caroline smiled and held his face in her hand.

"A special breakfast for a special day and special boys," she told him.

"We're ready for the surprise," Timmy said, looking from his mother to James. His face was covered by a large toothy smile. "Are we going to help in the fields? Are we going to work?"

"Maw, who's going to do the chores if we are working this morning?" Tommy asked as he put food into his mouth.

Timmy looked at him and frowned.

"Who do you think will do the chores?" he answered. "We still have to do our usual work. It's our job! Maw doesn't stop doing cooking, wash, and housecleaning just because Granny and her plant the gardens. We can't stop either."

Tommy nodded but said nothing. Soon he was finished with his breakfast and waited for Timmy to finish. When the boys came in from the morning chores, James met them at the door.

"Okay, Timmy, you guessed right. You get your chance at farming," he said with a laugh. "Your grandfather is a little tired so today you are going to help me work in the fields."

"Wow! Yes, yes! This is what I want to do!" came the answers from both boys.

James looked sternly at them. "It's not going to be easy. You will be tired when we get through with the day. I hope you can take it."

"We can take it!" Tommy exclaimed.

"We'll see, we'll see," was James' answer, winking at Caroline.

Caroline sat on the porch and watched as the boys followed James. He moved the plow behind the horse as rows were made. The twins picked up the exposed rocks and carried them to the edge of the creek.

A movement caught her eye and she turned to see who was walking toward them. It was Thom and Sarah. Thom continued toward the field but Sarah turned and joined Caroline on the porch.

"Thom couldn't stand watching from the window," Sarah said as she sat down. "He wants to be out there so bad, but his legs just won't let him stay out and work like he used to do. The rheumatism is really getting him."

Caroline patted her mother-in-law's arm. "I'm glad he has help this year."

"Maybe the good lord knew what we needed and sent that young man," Sarah went on. "I been praying for help. Maybe that's why he came. God sent him."

Caroline stared at James, eyes wide. He had stopped to talk to Thom. The boys had also stopped, but they were throwing dirt clods at each other.

"The boys have been praying, too," she finally said. "They've been praying for a father and...and a husband for me."

Sarah turned toward Caroline with a smile. "Those boys," she said shaking her head, "those boys are so sweet. I guess they are growing up and need help learning how to cope. A father would be helpful."

Caroline didn't answer. She turned her attention back to James. He was pointing to the boys and they were picking up more rocks. Thom stood close by and pointed where he wanted the rocks to be placed.

At noon, Caroline stood up and helped Sarah to get to her feet. They made a meal of cold potatoes, slices of ham, and bread. Taking it out to the field, Caroline spread a quilt on the ground and waited for the foursome to wash their hands in the creek.

"We almost have this field ready to plant," James told her as he sat down.

Caroline nodded and poured water for each of them.

"He sure is doin' a fine job out there," Thom said, grunting as he sat down. "He's gonna have that field ready by the first of the week. I'll have my strength back by then and be able to help him with the north end. By the end of May we should have the whole thing planted. Ain't that somethin'? He's a good worker."

"I appreciate the compliments, sir, but I have to say the boys have been a blessing. They have worked hard this morning," James said, head down.

"How are you boys doing?" Sarah asked as she set out sandwiches.

"I thought we would get to plow," Tommy grumbled. Looking at his hands, he grimaced at the blisters that had formed.

"I will put lard on your hands when we go in this evening," Caroline assured him as she also looked at his hands.

James reached over and rubbed his head. Then he took the boy's chin in his hand.

"I think when we go over the field this next time you boys might get your chance to help me. The ground is getting mighty soft with it being wet, so I might need to lead the horse while you hold the plow so it will go straight."

"Oh, boy! Me and Timmy can do that! Wait and see, we can do that!" Tommy yelled as he grabbed a sandwich.

James also picked up a sandwich. "What will be in this field?"

"That will be for the potatoes, turnips, onions, cabbage, and other early crops," Thom answered, taking out a piece of ham and putting it on a slice of bread. "It's still too early for the others to be planted."

"I forgot that's what you told me, Thom," James replied. "I guess we'll take one field at a time and get them plowed. This is a long strip of valley. How far back do you go?"

Caroline looked away from the quilt and pointed up the creek.

"You see that big rock up there where everything looks a little green? That's where the farmland goes. That green up there is wheat that survived the winter. When it dries, Sarah and I will make it into flour. There's also a fence around it. There's other grass that will be coming up soon. The gate will be closed and the sheep will be moved out there."

"Yes, sir, that's a good wheat field. The women make good flour out of it. When the corn is ready they will make cornmeal," Thom put in. 'And the cotton will make fine shirts for us to wear."

"You have every thing you need here," James slowly said. "What a great way of life. You have your own little store living right here between these two mountains. You don't need the rest of the world."

"Yep, we have what we need. We don't need outsiders except for the peddler. He brings what we can't grow or raise," Thom agreed, nodding. "And, he brings news that we need without us having to leave and get it. Yep, we can sit back and relax while the rest of the world does what it wants to do."

Caroline stared at the men for a moment. Anger filled her as she turned her attention to her own thoughts.

The rest of the world...the rest of the world that destroyed the peace and tranquility of her home when it went to war. The rest of the world that was rebuilding after the war that destroyed her family. The rest of the world that would take years to recover but could never restore her life back to the way it was.

"Caroline? Caroline do you want me to help you carry these things in?" Sarah asked as she touched Caroline's arm.

Caroline jumped. She looked at Sarah but her eyes wouldn't focus.

"Honey, are you all right?"

"I…I…yes, I'm fine. I was just lost in thought for a moment. That's all. I'm fine now," Caroline answered. Shaking her head, she looked at the quilt she was sitting on. The men and boys had left. "I…I think I do need your help with the dishes. I do feel somewhat tired. Thank you, Sarah."

"It's been a warm day," Sarah began, "You've been outside all morning. Maybe you need to go inside and rest for a while."

"No…no, I'm all right. We can get the dishes picked up and put in the basket. I'll take them in and wash them later. We can sit in the shade and watch the boys plow. That will be an interesting sight to see."

"That sounds fine to me," Sarah answered with a shrug. "I'm always happy to see what those boys get into. And, I need to keep an eye on Thom to make sure he doesn't do too much."

The shade was cool and refreshing. Caroline felt her heart calming, her mind clearing.

"You were right, Sarah, I do feel better now. I must have gotten too hot out there," she said as she watched the boys struggle with the plow. Thom was by their side helping guide it along.

"Those boys are trying so hard," Sarah laughed. "They are going to be so tired tonight."

"I'm glad they can rest tomorrow. Just look how they are straining. Their poor little bodies are going to be hurting."

"Those boys are stronger than you think, Caroline. They will be just fine," Sarah comforted.

Nodding, Caroline smiled as she watched her sons push as hard as they could against the plow as it moved along the furrows behind the horse.

Yes, they were strong. They would make fine men when they grew up. They would be independent and self-reliant. They would be able to take care of themselves.

Caroline wasn't sure if she was ready for them to grow-up.

Chapter 24

Yesterday was the bestest day!" Tommy yelled as he ran to do his morning chores. After milking the cow, he let the cow and calf into the corral. Watching them for a minute he began to dance around. Suddenly, he jumped up and clicked his heels.

"Ole Bessie gave us milk to drink, milk to drink, milk to drink," he suddenly started singing.

Timmy put his hands over his ears and started yelling at his brother.

"You can't sing!" he shouted. "You sing like you have a bucket on your head! Stop singing! Stop singing and I will milk the cow tomorrow!"

Tommy stopped and grinned. Whistling, he nodded and walked toward the house.

"I hope we get to do farmin' agin! I love to pick up the rocks! And, that old horse went straight down the rows just like he was supposed to do! We did as good as Grampa!"

Timmy looked at his brother and frowned. "We didn't do as good as Grampa. He had to help us keep the plow from falling over. And, it wasn't fun, it was work. Look at our hands. We have blisters," he said flatly. "It might have been a little bit of fun but it was mostly work. I was really tired when we came in last night."

"Yes, you were," Caroline agreed. "Your face was almost in your plate before you finished eating. I had to hold on to your hands to put grease on those blisters. You kept trying to lay your head on them."

"Hahaha, you couldn't keep your eyes open!" Tommy chirped.

Caroline turned to him and raised her brows. "Do you remember going to bed, young man?"

Laughter left Tommy. He looked around the room. He tried to remember, but couldn't.

Caroline smugly smiled at him. "Let me answer that for you. No, you probably don't and the reason for that is because Mr. Cartwright carried you to bed. You fell asleep at the table. I doctored your hands after he put you to bed."

Tommy lowered his head, and then raised it. "I guess I was tired too."

"You may have been tired but you boys did a fine job yesterday," James commented. "I think when we get ready for the other fields I will have some experienced help out there."

"Even with the plowin'?" Tommy asked with a gigantic smile.

"Even with the plowing," James answered.

"If Paw was here he would be very proud of us!' Timmy blurted out. "He would let us work with him every year from now on."

"I wish he was here. I...I think I miss him. I would like to tell him how good we did," Tommy slowly said.

James choked and looked at the floor in front of his chair.

Caroline looked from one boy to the other. It had been a long time since they had expressed emotions about their father. She felt the pain run through her. Quickly, she pulled herself under control. Hugging the boys, she smiled.

"He would be very proud of the work you are doing. You have really taken charge and stepped up. I'm also proud of you and I know Grampa and Granny are, too. Now come on, this is a good day. We are not going to let anything spoil it for us," she whispered.

Quietly, the boys sat up the checkers and began to play. Looking at each other, they hurriedly put them away and ran to their mother.

Caroline didn't realize they were by her side for a moment. When she did she started talking to them.

"This pie will use the last of the dried apples," Caroline said as she put crust into a pan. "All the fresh apples have been eaten, too. So, boys, don't ask for apples after today. This one is special because it celebrates all the hard work all of you have done."

"My favorite is apple but we still have canned berries, don't we?" Tommy shouted.

"Tommy, you don't have to raise your voice," his mother scolded. "Yes, we still have blackberries. There's a jar or two left from last year's picking."

"Then we don't have to worry," he answered. "We still have pie makings."

Laughter filled the room. Shaking her head, Caroline went back to making the pie. Soon the house began to fill with the aroma of hot sugary apples.

"Maw, I can see Grampa out at the fields. Can we go out there? And if he will watch us, can we go out to the crick? We might find a big fish in the deep hole."

"Well, I guess it will be all right. But don't go anywhere else. Make sure your grampa knows he is to watch you."

Saturday was usually a day of work but every one needed rest. Caroline didn't mind the boys taking the day off. She was going to do some wash and then she herself was going to take the afternoon off. As she turned from the stove, she noticed James sitting by the window looking out. He was solemn and didn't take interest in the boys running around the outside of the house. She also thought about how he had moved the food around in his plate at breakfast and eaten little of it.

Coming in from doing a load of wash, Caroline was surprised that James was still sitting in the same position. Relaxing in her rocker, she closed her eyes and was soon asleep.

Opening her eyes, she realized the boys were playing checkers on the rug.

"How long have you been in the house?" she asked.

"About an hour," Timmy answered. "You were asleep and Mr. Cartwright was just sitting quietly looking at a book. We didn't want to disturb you."

"That was mighty nice of you. What about your grampa? Did he go inside?"

"Yeah, we didn't see any fish so he said it was getting warm in the sun. We walked back up here with him."

Tommy's eyes lit up. "I walked him home just like you have us to do. He said he appreciated it."

"That was nice of you, Tommy," Caroline said with a big smile. She winked at Timmy.

"Boys, I need fresh water from the well. Do you think the two of you can bring some in without spilling most of it?"

"Yes, ma'am," Timmy answered as he grabbed a piece of bread from the table. "Come on, Tommy. I'll race you out there."

"Timmy, both of you get a pail for water! We will eat dinner in a little while. I'll set the left over chicken and boiled potatoes out in an hour or so and then we will have a nice warm meal tonight. And, boys, be careful at the well. Don't get to playing while you are out there. Keep your eyes and ears open."

"Yes, ma'am," Timmy answered. Stopping, he turned around and cocked his head. "Maw, can we go out and look at the field we plowed? I want to see the furrows."

Nodding, Caroline replied with a weak smile, "Yes, but don't run around in the plowed ground. We don't want to have to make rows again. And don't stay out there too long. I need that water in the house. Oh, oh, and go ask your granny if she needs water, too."

She watched as the door slammed and the whoops faded.

James didn't move from the chair he was in. He watched as the boys put on their boots.

As the door closed, he stood up and moved to the kitchen.

"Caroline, I need to talk to you. Would you please sit down for a few minutes?"

"Well...well, I really need to get the stew on for supper tonight. Can't it wait? It shouldn't take me more than an hour to get everything prepared and have it on the stove."

James lowered his head and sighed. "I guess so. I've waited this long. I can wait a little longer."

Caroline saw the somber look in his eyes. Quietly, she sat down and stared at him.

Was he going to tell her he was leaving? Did he feel it was time?

James didn't raise his head. He gave another sigh.

"All right, James, I am listening. I guess the stew can be made a little later. What do you want to talk about?"

James stood up and walked around the room. His insides burned. There was an ache in his chest. Finally, he sat down again.

"Caroline, I haven't been truthful with you," he started. "You had every right to be mad at me when you found out I knew the boys' names. The truth is, I knew I wanted to see this place and you when I came up from Monticello."

Caroline frowned. Shaking her head, she opened her mouth. James placed his hand up before her.

"Please let me talk. I may not have the courage later. I've got to get this off my chest before I explode. You and the boys deserve to know the truth. I can't keep pretending any longer. The truth is, I knew your husband. I knew Thomas. I didn't know him when he was telling his stories about the mountains. I told you the truth about that. But near the end, we were in the same regiment. I'm sorry I didn't tell you sooner."

Caroline gasped. Her throat closed. Her eyes burned.

James stopped and closed his eyes for a moment.

"The truth is…the truth is, he had made corporal before Gettysburg. I also was raised in my rank. I told you we had lost lots of men. Our regiment was in need of men to lead. At Gettysburg we were to hold a hill. We were spread out thin. Our orders were to stay put and wait for the enemy to come to us. We waited and could hear cannon fire. It came closer and closer. Realization hit that the other regiments fighting at Gettysburg were falling all around us. It didn't take long for the union soldiers to be on us. The men I was with fought gallantly. The battle was fierce. Suddenly, Thomas was in front of me. A ball hit him and he fell. As I moved to check on him I was hit in the side. I fell beside him."

James's face paled. His hands shook. His eyes looked far away, far into the past.

"Thomas…your husband…was badly injured. He…he was gut shot. There was nothing I could do but be by his side."

James stopped and looked at the woman sitting across from him. "Caroline, you were his life. He loved you with every breath in his body. He loved you to the end."

Caroline jumped up and backed against the pie safe. Throwing her hand to her mouth, she whimpered. Anger overcame her. Her face began to burn.

"You lied to me! You said you only heard him talk about his love of this place. How could you stay here and act like you didn't know him and that you knew nothing about what happened at Gettysburg! How could you pretend in front of his parents? How could you do this to his children? How could you do this to *me?* How could you! Get out! Get out now! I never want to see you again!"

James looked into Caroline's eyes and then closed his. Shaking his head he got up and started to put on his coat. Stopping, he looked at it for moment and then hung it back on the nail. He couldn't take the coat. It belonged to Thomas.

Turning back to Caroline, James spoke again.

"I'm sorry. I'm really sorry. I didn't mean any harm. When I came here I was going to tell you but after I met you and the boys, I couldn't get the words out. I fell in love with the boys. I'm sorry. I won't bother you again if that is what you really want. Caroline, please -- "

"Get out!" Caroline cried. "Don't ever come back! You are a liar! A liar can't be trusted! You keep lying to me! I don't know what to believe anymore! Get out!"

"I've never lied to you, Caroline. I...I've just had...had –."

"Get out!"

James closed the door behind him as Caroline slid to the floor. Grabbing her apron, she covered her face. Pain spread through her. An unbearable ache took over.

It felt like an hour before the door opened again. Timmy and Tommy came in and pulled off their boots.

"Maw, where was Mr. Cartwright going? He hugged us and then saddled his horse and rode off," Timmy asked. "Why are you on the floor?"

"I...I slipped, but I'm all right now. You boys get the checkers out and play."

"But where was Mr. Cartwright going? Is he going to meet the peddler?" Timmy asked

Caroline looked at the floor. She was numb. Finally, she was able to answer.

"He remembered that he had to go back home. He...he won't be back. He enjoyed the visit but his time here is over."

The words were bitter in her mouth. She hated lying to the boys. She didn't want to teach them it was all right to not tell the truth.

"I'm going to miss him," Tommy said with his head on the table.

"Me, too," Timmy added. "I was hoping he would be our paw."

Caroline couldn't look at the boys. Someday she might tell them what happened. Someday, if she thought they could handle the truth.

Chapter 25

A light rain began to fall as night came. Caroline had forgotten about the stew. She dished up warmed over beans and cornbread to the boys. They sat and ate quietly. They knew something was wrong but were afraid to ask.

Caroline still was quiet when it was time for bed. She listened to the boys' prayers but didn't add to them. Kissing them goodnight, she walked over to her rocking chair and sat down. Pulling her shawl around her, she soon could hear the boys' easy breathing as they fell asleep.

The house grew cold as Caroline stared at the dying embers in the fireplace. She couldn't will herself to move. She had sat in front of the fire all night. Sleep wouldn't come.

"Maw, I'm cold," Timmy said at her elbow as daylight broke over the hills. "Can I put a log on the fire?"

Caroline continued to stare. A tear fell on her blouse.

"Maw!" Tommy exclaimed. "Maw, the fire is dying! We need more wood on the fire! It's cold in here. Ma, are you going to make something to eat?"

No response.

Timmy picked up several small sticks and put them in the fireplace. Using one, he stirred the ashes. The coals sparked and glowed. Soon the sticks began to catch fire.

"Maw, how many logs do I put in?" Timmy asked. "Is it one or two?"

A knock at the door halted the exchange. Tommy crossed to the door and opened it. Thom shook rain from his coat and stepped in.

"Got chilly last night," Thom said as he looked around. "Have a little frost on the ground and windows this morning. I didn't see much smoke coming from the chimney. Something wrong with the draw?"

"Maw hasn't put any logs on. It's getting cold and all she is doing is sitting there," Tommy answered as he pointed in his mother's direction.

Thom looked in Caroline's direction then back at the boys.

"Have the animals been checked this morning?"

"No, we've been in here trying to get Maw to talk to us," Timmy answered. "Maw hasn't built the fire and she hasn't fixed breakfast. She doesn't answer when we talk to her either."

Thom moved forward and gazed at Caroline. Taking off his coat, he laid it across a chair and continued forward.

"Boys, go out and make sure the animals have plenty of water and check the hay. Go on, scoot. I'll take care of the fire," he said as he moved toward the hearth.

"Can we have a biscuit?" Tommy asked. "My stomach is growling."

"Yeah, yeah," Thom answered without looking in their direction. His eyes were fixed on Caroline.

Shrugging, the boys grabbed a biscuit, hurried into their coats and boots, and left.

Thom placed logs into the fireplace. Stoking the fire he watched as the embers of the small sticks caught and began to glow. Finally, he sat down next to Caroline and cocked his head.

"Caroline, are you all right?"

"He lied to me, Thom," Caroline said as another tear slid down her cheek. "He knew he was on this land. He knew who we were. He knew Thomas! He lied, he lied, *he* lied!"

"I know."

Caroline stared at Thom. Disbelief filled her. Her heart began to pound. Her breathing shallowed.

"You knew? How? Why didn't you say something?"

"He told me the whole story the day we went down to meet the peddler. Caroline, he wanted to tell you. He said he tried but he couldn't."

Thom reached out and took her hand. Gently rubbing it, he looked carefully at her.

"Caroline, I need to know how you feel. I don't mean about him not telling you the truth, but how you feel about James."

Caroline turned back to the fire. The flames danced around the logs.

How do I feel? I feel angry! Distrust! Violated! Caroline wanted to scream. Taking a deep breath, she tried to calm herself. Turning her thoughts to James, she tried to separate her feelings.

"I feel…I feel hurt. He was so good to the boys. They adore him. If they ever found out that he knew their father –

"And, what is wrong with them finding out that he knew their father? Caroline, you don't know the whole story. You don't know what the man went through. You can't imagine what drove him to come here. Don't you think you owe that to him?"

"How can you forgive him!" Caroline lashed out. "He knew Thomas and acted like it was nothing. *Nothing!*"

"Caroline, I have nothing to forgive him for. He was in the same war Thomas was in. He was in the same battle. He can't help it if he lived and my son didn't. It isn't his fault. No, Caroline, I can't blame him. It was war. They both could have been killed. He's a good man, a really good man."

Caroline stood and walked around the room. A tear formed.

"Do you love him, Caroline?" Thom gently formed the words. He could see the young woman wince. He knew the answer. "Have you let him into your heart just as the boys have?"

Pounding her fist into her open hand, Caroline continued to pace. Shaking her head, her eyes were glazed. The pain in her heart wouldn't stop.

"Caroline, what would you like to do?" Thom asked as he watched the turmoil on his daughter-in-law's face.

"It doesn't matter. It's too late now. He's gone. I told him not to ever come back. He's probably out of the county by now. I don't even know where he was going."

Thom moved toward her and hugged her close. Her face buried into his shoulder. Finally, he held her by the shoulders and looked at her.

"It's never too late to let someone know how you feel about them. Honey, he isn't gone. He's at our house. He's been there ever since he left here yesterday. Caroline, he is about destroyed. You need to talk to him. You need to listen to what he has to say before you judge him. It's the least you can do."

Caroline stared at Thom.

"He's at your house? But…but –"

"He started to leave. He got as far as where the crick makes the bend before going through the woods. Then he turned back and stopped at our cabin. Caroline, he is a broken man. The war almost killed him. You need to listen to him. Really listen to him."

Caroline stared at Thom. She couldn't believe he was taking James's side. He should have been as angry as she was.

Thom took her in his arms again. Kissing her on the forehead, he nodded at her.

"Caroline, go to him. I will stay here with the boys. I'll be in the shed with the boys when you are ready to leave. The boys and I will be fine here. Now you get your things together."

"Wait! I haven't set out anything to eat. The boys will be hungry," she said as she moved toward the kitchen.

"Don't worry about that. I know how to make oats and believe it or not, I know how to make biscuits. The boys will not starve. I can take care of it." Thom answered with a laugh. "Now, you get a move on."

"There are biscuits already made. They are on the table. I have boiled potatoes in a bucket across the dog run. You can cut some ham over there if you want."

"Honey, it's breakfast time. I can fix breakfast. Now scoot, you are wasting time. He might decide to leave. You need to get going."

Caroline hurried to her room. Grabbing her work coat, a cap, and gloves, she hurried toward the shed.

"Boys, you mind your grandfather. I will be back in a little while. Don't make any trouble," she said as Thom put his hands on the boy's shoulders.

"They will be just fine, Caroline. I know how to take care of them," Thom answered with a chuckle. "You just take care of business. We'll see you when you return."

Mud filled Caroline's boots as she tried to run across it. She couldn't move fast. Her skirt dragged in the slushy muck and held her back.

Lord, let him still be there when I arrive, Caroline prayed as she followed the small trail.

Fog filled the little valley. She could only see a short distance in front of her. She could smell the wood burning before she could see the smoke from the chimney. Dogs barked and met her as she came into view of the house. She stopped near a fencepost that was part of the old fence. She thought she could see James's horse near the end of the house. Turning toward the house, she reached out and opened the gate. Moving with more determination she walked faster, splashing through puddles of water along the path.

The door swung open as she reached it. Sarah stood just inside.

"Is…is…is he still here?" Caroline stammered.

Sarah smiled and motioned for the nervous woman to come in.

Caroline stepped inside and saw James sitting in a chair by the fireplace. His face was in his hands.

"James," she quietly said.

No response.

"James, I'm here to listen."

Still, no response.

Caroline looked at Sarah and then back at James. Walking over to him, she stood in front of him.

"James, I want to hear what you have to say. I was wrong to not listen to what you had to say. I will listen if you will give me another chance to do so. I want to know everything."

James looked up. His face was red and drawn.

"Are you sure? Do you really want to hear?"

Caroline sank to the floor in front of him. "Yes, yes, I do want to hear what happened on the battlefield. I want to know what you and...and Thomas did in...in...in his last moments."

Caroline closed her eyes and bit her lip. Pressure pushed at her chest. An ache filled her heart. She knew the worst was yet to come.

Chapter 26

Sarah quietly sat down at the table and fiddled with the dishtowel in front of her. She also wanted to hear what James had to say. It had been her baby boy that had fought and died near him.

James's head moved from side to side. His body became limp. It shuttered.

Caroline slowly sat down beside James. Her eyes were moist; her breathing heavy. She placed her hand on his arm.

"James, I want to know about what happened at Gettysburg. I need to know what happened. I can't leave the past in the past if I don't know what happened."

Caroline knew her sentences didn't sound coherent but it didn't matter. She hoped James understood what she was trying to say.

The man beside her lowered his face again and then raised it. Staring at the fireplace, he wiped his face on his sleeve.

His body ached. His mind filled with the battle scene. The noise echoed through him and then quiet serenity replaced it all. His mouth began to move.

"I held my hands on him. I tried to stop the bleeding but it wouldn't stop. I kept yelling for help but no one came. I tried to save him, Caroline! I really tried!"

James's breath caught. Sweat began to edge his brow. A shutter came from deep within.

"We talked. He told me about his…this wonderful family; about playing music on holidays and at the end of harvest. He missed the times when it was just him, his brother Joseph, and his father sitting out there on the porch while Sarah sat in her rocker and smiled. He said he missed his mother and her sweet disposition. He hated that he didn't hug and kiss her one last time before he rode off to join the army. He said he wished he could eat one more piece of her fried chicken with fried potatoes and big slices of onion on the side."

Sarah sniffled and pulled her apron to her face. Her face was pale and her hands trembled.

James took a deep breath and continued. "After a while, all he talked about was you and the children. He told me about the boys and the joy they gave him. He wanted to teach them to play music and how to whittle. He wanted them to learn to hunt and respect the land and what it provided for survival. He loved the mountains but he didn't feel it could offer enough in the way of prospering. He wanted more for the boys than what he had. He wanted them to be part of the growth he envisioned in Arkansas; the growth and prosperity."

James stopped again and wiped tears. Swallowing hard, he wiped his nose. Blinking, he continued.

"He also explained how he had moved you up here near his parents when the regiment was forming. But mostly, but mostly, Caroline, he talked about you. He talked about how you looked in the mornings while you sang and made breakfast and how you played with… the boys. He longed to hold you and tell you how much he loved you. He couldn't wait to get home to see his…his…new daughter that was born just a few months before he left."

Caroline gasped. Tears slid down her face.

James took another deep breath. His throat had a knot in it. He tried to swallow it but it wouldn't go down.

His eyes were fixed on the floor. His mind was in another place, another time. He could see the dying man on the ground in front of him; the man covered in his own blood moving his hands along his coat.

"He tried hard to pull something from his pocket but he was getting weaker and weaker. Finally, he told me to reach in and pull out the items he was trying to get. I pulled out two knives."

James shook his head.

"The...the knives you put in the boys' socks?" Caroline feebly asked.

James nodded. "He told me there was a doll in his bedroll. I had his head resting on it. He raised his head and asked that I get it."

James rubbed his hands for a few minutes. Gritting his teeth, he closed his eyes.

"I slowly laid his head on my leg and pulled the blanket from under his head. He reached over and slowly unrolled it and pulled the doll out. The blood...the blood —

Reaching over, James picked up his own bedroll and placed it on his lap. Slowly, he began to unroll it. The small rag doll fell out.

Caroline picked up the doll and held it near her face. Light red stains covered the little rag doll she held.

"I tried to wash the blood off but it wouldn't come out."

Tears filled Sarah's eyes. She wanted to run to Caroline but her feet were rooted to the floor.

"I crawled to a tree that had a small hole where the roots went into the ground. I hid the knives and doll in the hole after.... I didn't know if they would be sent to you or not. I didn't even know if I would live to bring them to you, but I didn't want the Union soldiers to get their hands on them. I dug them out when I…when I got out of prison back in the summer."

"That's why you came here? You came to bring these things to us?"

Caroline's eyes widened. She looked around the room. Turning, she looked at Sarah. Their eyes met and Caroline felt the pain the older woman was feeling.

"That's a big part of the reason," James said, pulling his hands down his face, "but I also came because of you."

"Me? How could I be a reason for you to come here?"

Sarah got up from the table and picked up her shawl.

"I think I'm going to check on Grampa and the boys," she quietly said. "I think I need to get some fresh air and let you two talk alone."

Slowly she moved to Caroline's side, patted her shoulder, and left the cabin.

"Would you like to explain to me how I had anything to do with you coming here?" Caroline asked hoarsely. Slowly, she sank into Sarah's rocking chair.

James nodded and pulled the leather pouch out of his blanket. Carefully, he pulled the bloody, folded letter out.

"Thomas also had this letter. I know I shouldn't have read it because it was to him, but he asked me to read it. He said...he said you were full of love and tenderness. You deserved happiness and be given more love than he ever gave you. He...he wished he had told you more how much he loved you."

Caroline's mouth opened but nothing came out. Breathing became hard. Her head swirled.

James's words reverberated through her. Every nerve burned, then numbed.

"Caroline, are you all right?" James asked. Concern filled him. *Had he said too much?*

"I...I...I think..." Caroline tried to gulp in air. Finally, her head began to clear.

"He...he did tell me he loved me. He told me all the time, even in his letters," she choked out. Slowly, she calmed her fast heart and gained control again. "What happened next, James? I want to know."

James closed his eyes and deeply sighed.

"He died before I could open the letter. I put it in my pocket and covered him with his blanket. I said another prayer and then waited for the Yankees to arrive. It wasn't ...it wasn't until I was placed in prison that I read it. I had it hidden away in my boot before I was taken from the battlefield. After I was stitched up and taken to an empty spot on the ground where the confederate soldiers were placed, I worried that it would be found. But, thank the good lord, it wasn't. A few weeks later, we were taken by train to Delaware. I was imprisoned at Camp Dover. Caroline, your letter kept me alive. I was in prison for almost four years. I read your letter every day. I dreamed of having someone back home that loved me as much as you loved your husband. I dreamed of someone waiting for me to return. I needed that to survive."

"You...you were in a Union prison that long?"

Nodding, James rubbed his face and hair again. Another long sigh escaped.

"Yes. The prison was on an island in Delaware. I had it better than the regular enlisted men but not much. It was cold and damp. The food was sparse. The smell was unbearable. Saying it was miserable doesn't describe what it was like. It was a living hell. Sometimes I wished I had died during the battle. It would have been better than being where I was. But then I would read your letter. I thought about what Thomas Hollister had said. I thought of the love you had to give. I guess...I guess I daydreamed too much. I came to believe...it doesn't matter anymore. It was just a dream. I'm so sorry, Caroline for all the hurt I put you through."

"I," Caroline started, "I don't know what to say."

"You don't have to say anything. I understand I put you through too much. I'll be leaving in a few minutes," James got up and placed the letter into her hand. "After meeting you, I can see why Thomas fell in love with you. I…I also have really fallen in love with you. It's not a dream anymore. I hope you lots of happiness. You deserve it. Some man will come along and make you very happy. He will be able to fill your heart with love again."

Turning back to his blanket, James began to roll it again.

Caroline sat stunned. The letter was soft in her hand. Looking down, she stared at the blood soaked paper.

"James, I…,"

"It's all right. I understand."

"No, you don't," Caroline finally got out. "I have some things to say, too. You already know that Thomas and I had a daughter. He told you and…and I may have mentioned it when I was talking about the men that came here. She…she died of pneumonia during the winter of '63. She's buried in the graveyard up on the ridge. I almost lost Tommy that year, too. It was hard; real hard. If it hadn't been for Thom and Sarah I don't know what I would have done.

"I missed Thomas so much. I threw myself into making a home for the boys and myself. I had convinced myself that we could make a life for ourselves without any outside help. We had Thom and Sarah and Thomas's brother and sister. We didn't need anyone else.

When you came…when you came, something began to stir in me. It's been a long time; I've been a widow a long time. I was afraid to feel anything. Out in the shed; well, I didn't know how to handle the feelings that were stirring."

James locked his eyes on her. Cocking his head, he let his heart talk.

"Caroline…,"

"No, let me finish. I…I was afraid of the feelings. I felt I was betraying Thomas. I couldn't let that happen. I wanted you to leave, but at the same time, I wanted you to stay. I told myself it was good for the boys and that you staying just through the winter would be all right. I was wrong. Their feelings for you have kept growing. When they came to me with their crazy idea about you and me, about us…well…well…I told them it could never happen. I rationalized the whole situation. I didn't plan… if you… uh… feelings… uh… sorry… I didn't intend to lead you on."

Sobs came. Caroline tried to control them but couldn't. A weight filled her chest. The pit of her stomach burned and caved in. Cold ran up her spine followed by a burning fire that raged through her skin along her arms.

James tried to console her but his own emotions got in the way. His hands wouldn't move from his sides. Finally, he knelt in front of the rocking chair and forced his hand to move to hers.

"Caroline, you didn't. I...I fell in love with you before I ever came here. I know it sounds crazy, but I fell in love with you by reading your letter. I didn't mean to. In fact, I told myself that I would bring the knives and doll up here and then go on to Mountain Home and try to get a teaching position. That part was true. But then the snow and ice kept me here. I prayed to God for the ice to melt so I could leave. I didn't intend to stay. I didn't want to get attached to the boys. I didn't want my heart to get hurt and...and I didn't want to hurt you. I must have been mad when you asked me to stay through the winter and I agreed. I don't know what came over me. I should have left."

"None of it makes since. I don't know what happened. But, James, I know one thing, I prayed, too. I wanted God's will to be done. James, I think it has been his will all along. I...I think I've fallen in love with you. I don't want you to leave. I want you to stay so we can see if it is love. Will you stay?"

James pulled Caroline from the chair and held her hands as they stood.

"Are you sure? I can leave right now and you'll never have to see me again. I'll understand if you say you want me to leave."

"I'm sure. I want you to stay. The boys...James, the boys have been praying for a father. They told me so. It...it...would be unfair to them if their prayers have been answered and...and we messed it up. We need to make sure for their sake."

James put his hand to the small of Caroline's back and pulled her closer. Lowering his head, he placed his lips on hers.

Pulling away, he looked deep into her eyes.

"I want you to stay," she whispered as a tear slid down her cheek.

"You don't know how much I want to stay. Caroline, I love those boys so much. They are like my own. I don't ever want to do anything that would hurt them. I don't want to do anything that would ever hurt you again. I love you so much."

Nodding, Caroline moved her face close to his once again as he took her in his arms.

Chapter 27

The fog had lifted, Caroline noted, when she opened the door. The dogs were quiet and only the screech of a hawk occasionally broke the subdued hollow. She could hear the stream moving quickly down toward the opening. The water would soon be part of the larger creek that ran through the large valley outside their little hollow.

Looking toward her cabin, she could see smoke coming from the chimney. She knew Sarah had gone down there and was with the boys and Thom.

"I know you were emotional inside," James said as he closed the door behind them. "It's not too late to tell me to leave. The boys would never have to know I haven't left yet."

Caroline turned and faced him.

"I said I don't want you to leave. The boys…no, I won't use that as an excuse anymore…I want you to stay for me, for us. It would be a mistake to let you ride away and then regret it for the rest of our lives."

Relief filled James. Nodding, he walked down the steps behind her.

Caroline stepped over puddles and reached the path leading toward her cabin. Stopping, she looked at the hillside and then back toward the house.

"I want to go up to the ridge," she said. "We can go to the cabin afterwards."

James looked at the mountain and then back at Caroline. Puzzled, he raised his brows.

"I...I want you to meet someone," Caroline let out, closing her eyes. "I want you to meet Alice."

Holding James's hand, Caroline walked along a narrow path toward the top of the ridge behind her in-laws' cabin. In her other hand she held the faded doll.

"We are almost there," she said as she took another step.

"Are you sure you want me to be here?" James asked.

Smiling Caroline looked at him and nodded. "I think she would be happy to see you," she replied. Lifting her hand, she handed him the doll. "I think you should give her the doll and tell her about her father."

James cleared his throat and took the doll. Looking up he could see a clearing up ahead. Several grave markers were standing in the patch of cleared ground. Grave markers, that were rocks standing on end, with a small wooden fence around them.

James recognized the spot. He had seen it before.

With a squeeze of her hand, Caroline led him along the sides of the graves.

"This is where Thomas's grandparents are buried," she said as she moved along, "and this is Joseph, his brother, and there are a couple of other graves where a brother or sister was stillborn and buried."

Kneeling, she looked at the carved rock in front of her. Dead flowers, with wilted stems still buried in the ground, were in front of it. Slowly she removed them and threw them a short distance away.

James could see the words 'Alice Hollister' carved into the rock. There was a date but it was more faded than the name.

"This is Alice," Caroline said, caressing the stone. "This is my beautiful daughter. I miss her so much."

James could see the tears glistening as they ran down her cheeks. He wanted to reach out and catch them, but refrained. They were her tears: tears for the years that she didn't get to spend with her daughter; tears of hurt and longing.

Kneeling beside her, he placed the doll in front of the stone.

"It's nice to meet you, Alice," he quietly said. "I heard a lot about you from your father. He loved you very much. He would like to have been here but…but a war got in the way. He had this gift for you. He sent it with all his love. He knew it would be something you would cherish."

James turned away. He couldn't see through the mist that clouded his own vision. Sniffling, he blinked his eyes, and then wiped them on his sleeve. Again he looked at the girl's name on the rock.

"I know it took a long time to get your doll here but there were reasons behind that. I wish you could have gotten it years ago, but I'm glad I got to bring it to you now even though…."

James didn't finish the sentence. He couldn't. He suddenly realized he loved the girl that he had never met. He loved her because her mother and father loved her. He loved her because her brothers loved her and had played with her.

Touching the name on the stone, James gently rubbed it.

"I want to be part of your life. I want to take care of your mother and brothers. I promise to be good to them and love them with my whole heart. I want your approval."

A slight breeze whipped up a leaf and it landed on James' shoulder. Looking up he took Caroline's hand.

"I'm going to take that as a sign that she approves," he said with a wide grin.

Caroline smiled back. "I think there are four more down at the cabin who will give their approval also. Are you ready to go down to see them?"

"Caroline let's pray before we go down. I want everyone's blessing when we tell them our decisions."

Caroline turned to him and nodded. "I think that is what we should do. I also want to thank the lord for intervening."

Timmy was getting a drink of water from the dipper in the water bucket when he saw the couple walking toward the cabin.

"Mr. Cartwright didn't leave!" he shouted. Dropping the dipper back into the bucket, he ran for the door. "Maw is with him!"

Tommy jumped from the kitchen table he was sitting at. He almost beat his brother to the door.

Running to James, the boys almost knocked him down.

"Whoa! I need to stay on my feet," he laughed.

Thom stood behind his wife inside the doorway. His arm was around her.

"Are you going to stay?" Timmy asked, his face buried in James's side. "Please stay. I won't complain about Tommy not doing his work and I'll work extra hard."

"I promise to be good if'n you will stay. I will do everything you and Maw tell me to do without complaining. Please say you will stay!" Tommy pleaded.

James pulled the boys from his waist and looked at both. Hugging them close again, he laughed.

"Boys, I think you are perfect the way you are. You don't have to change just to keep me here either."

Caroline encircled the three standing beside her and smiled toward her in-laws.

"Boys, we need to talk to your grandparents. I want you to sit on the porch while we visit in the house. Will you do that for me?"

Tommy kept trying to see what was going on inside. He could see the mouths moving but couldn't hear any words.

Caroline stood in front of Thom and Sarah. Her mind was whirling. She wasn't sure what she was going to say to them.

"I guess you two have had a long talk. Is that right?" Thom asked.

Nodding, Caroline sat down at the table.

"Caroline, Thom and I have known for a while how James feels about you. We could see it in his face and hear it in his voice when he talked about you. We could also see how fond of the boys he is. We also know how you feel about him. We want what is best for you."

"You…you do?" Caroline sputtered out. "But…but, I thought you might feel that I was betraying Thomas."

"Betraying Thomas? Honey, Thomas has been gone a long time. You won't be betraying him. He wouldn't want you to be alone. He would want you and the boys to be happy."

Thom smiled at his wife then turned to Caroline and James.

"After you told me about the letter, I told Sarah about it. We both wondered if it was God who had our son give you that letter. He wanted Caroline to be taken care of and you were measured and shaken to be that man to take care of her. Thomas saw something in you, something good."

Caroline looked at James. He lifted his hand and placed it on her shoulder.

"When I prayed with your son, I prayed for his wife and children. I prayed for them to find peace and happiness. I do love Caroline and the boys. Any man would fall in love with them. They love the Lord with all their hearts and are a joy to be around," James said, looking at the older couple. "Thom, Sarah, could we ask for your blessings? We don't want to do anything that you wouldn't approve of."

Caroline put her hand on James's. Looking up at him she added, "And, there are a few other things we would like to talk to you about."

Finally, the door opened and Thom motioned for the twins to enter the house. Slowly they walked through the door and stood before their mother.

"You are the most wonderful sons a person could have," she said with a smile. "I'm not going to beat around the bush because I have a question to ask you. I would like to know how you would like James as your father. He…."

The boys screamed and grabbed each other.

"I knew it!" Timmy yelled, "I knew he loved Maw! I told you, I told you!"

"When will we get married?" Tommy added to the noise.

"Well, that is what we were talking to your grandparents about," Caroline answered, licking her bottom lip. "You see, James and I have talked about going back to south Arkansas. I want to see my family. I think they will be thrilled to see how much you have grown. We decided...."

Tommy stopped his jumping and stared at the grownups. Timmy's eyes grew wide and he stood silently beside his brother for just a moment then spoke.

"Leave here? You want to leave our home? But, Maw, Granny and Grampa need us! Who will kill squirrels, rabbits, and coons for them? Who will help plow and harvest?"

Sarah pulled Timmy close and put her arm around his shoulders.

"Maw...," Tommy began.

"Wait, boys, be fair. You need to let your mother finish," James spoke up.

Caroline started again. This time, she sat down close to the boys and held her hands for them to join her.

"As I was going to say, we have decided to make a trip to our homes in south Arkansas. We want to see our families. You will get to see your other set of grandparents and aunts and uncles. They will be so happy to see you, too. Once we get there we plan to marry. It will be a big family wedding with lots of cousins for you to meet."

"We have cousins here," Timmy argued, "We like seeing them."

"Yes, you do," Caroline answered, "But it would be nice to get to know your other cousins."

"I don't want to go!" Tommy screamed. Backing toward his grandfather, he grabbed his waist. "I want to stay here with Grampa!"

James held his hands up and laughed. "Wait, wait, boys, I think you are misunderstanding. We aren't planning to move to the Delta. We just plan to go down for a visit so I can meet your mother's family and she can meet mine. We are coming back to live here. We don't intend to take you away from your grandparents. We don't want to live anywhere else. This is the best home we could have. We can grow our own food, hunt for meat, and live in peace."

Caroline looked from one boy to the other. Slowly, she knelt in front of them. Taking the hand of each one, she spoke quietly.

"Boys, we don't have a preacher here. We need to go where there is one so we can get married proper. There is one in the delta where there are churches built for people to go to."

"You mean they don't have church in their home?" Timmy asked.

"No, most of the people go to one of the churches. They have a man who reads the bible and tells about it. He is called a preacher. He's the one who can marry your mother and me. People sing and there are classes where you boys can learn about the stories in the bible."

"Maw, we do that here. Grampa is our preacher. Granny teaches us the stories and we sing while Grampa plays the music. Couldn't Grampa marry you?"

Caroline smiled and hugged her son. "It is true your grampa is like a preacher and we will have that kind of church when we return. But, he can't marry us. We need an ordained preacher to marry James and me. So we will go to the delta to get married."

Whoops filled the large room as the boys started dancing and hugging everyone.

"Wait," Timmy said suddenly. "How long will we be gone?"

"About three months. We will be back before it's time to harvest most of the crops," James answered and then added. "We aren't leaving until I help your grampa get the fields planted. We will start plowing the ground again tomorrow. Do I have any takers in helping with the work?"

"Will you let me plow?" Tommy asked his grandfather with a big smile.

Thom hugged his wife and frowned.

"We'll have to see, Tommy, we'll have to see."

"I think you boys will have to start out moving rocks again. New field means more rocks to move," James said, patting the boy on the head.

Timmy groaned, looked up at the adults with a frown, and shook his head.

"Maw, if I am going to be a farmer, then I need gloves. Does the peddler have gloves?"

Laughter filled the room.

Caroline looked around the room. Her heart pounded. Joy filled her.

This is my family, she noted. *This is where I belong. I've wasted so much time wishing I was living my old life in the delta. I thought that life couldn't be replaced. How wrong I have been! I couldn't see what was before me because of my selfish thoughts. James and Thom are right. We have our own piece of the world right here. We don't need the outside world. We have each other.*

Chapter 28

Three Months Later

"We're home," Caroline said to her new husband as they entered the small wagon trail that led into the hollow. "I loved seeing my parents and brothers. They look so good. It was wonderful that the boys got to fish and picnic in the bayou with them just like I used to do.

"I can't believe there are such weird looking trees in the bayou! I never heard of trees having knees! And, I'm glad I got to see the flat land! I've never seen so much farmland!" Timmy said as he moved toward the front seat of the wagon. "It looks so different than here. Someday I hope we go back to visit. I want to see more of it."

Caroline hugged James's arm and smiled back at Timmy.

"I'm glad you got to see it, too. I'm sure we will make a few more trips back to see our families."

"Did you see the towns! They were real towns! I've never seen so many people!" Timmy continued. "Maw did we see all the towns that are in Arkansas?"

Laughing, Caroline patted Timmy's hand. "Oh Timmy, there are lots of large towns in Arkansas. We just saw part of them."

"There's lots more to the world than I could ever imagine," Timmy exclaimed as he shook his head. "I'm glad we left the holler and went to see Grandma and Grandpa on the plantation."

Turning to James, Caroline's smile got larger. "I'm glad I got to meet James's family, too. They were so nice to us. I feel like I've known them forever. But, James, oh James, I didn't realize until a few day ago how much the mountains have become my home. I know longer think of the delta as my home and I won't be longing to see it like I used to. I found myself comparing what I have here to what I thought I was missing there. I realize I'm not missing anything. My life is complete right here."

James hugged her and smiled. "I'm happy that we decided to stay here. I have nothing left in the delta. I signed what is left of my plantation over to my brothers. I have found what I need right here in the Ozarks. I found you and the boys. And, I found a new life. Those things are all I need. I've grown to love it here."

"I've always loved it," Tommy chimed in. "I can't remember living anywhere but in the holler. I wouldn't be happy living anywhere else. I love Granny and Grampa."

Looking back at the boys, James laughed. They were almost out of the woods and the little valley was looming in front of them.

Green fields greeted them on both sides of the creek. Tall corn waved, as did the wheat, as the wagon passed by. Large, lush, big leafed squash plants smiled at the sun. Long runners, from pumpkin plants, covered large areas of the ground.

Everyone stared at the lush green valley as they moved toward the cabins.

Tommy stood in the wagon and howled.

"I can't wait for the harvest to come in! Grampa said we would have a hoedown and play music. I hope Granny makes corn on the cob, fried fish, and lots of other stuff."

"I can't believe I'm saying it but I love the holler and I can't wait for the hoedown either," Timmy put in. "When I grow up I might live somewhere else but I will always come home and help with the harvest. This is where my heart will be."

Caroline hugged her son and shook her head. "Timmy, my sweet, level-headed son, how did I know you were going to say that!"

Timmy smiled. "Maw, you know everything!"

Caroline looked at James and took hold of his arm.

"Not everything," she whispered, "I almost made the biggest mistake I could have ever made. Thanks to my sons, my in-laws, and the Lord, I didn't. They are so much smarter than me."

James took her hand in his and smiled.

"I'm glad you listened to them and to your heart. I love you so much. I don't ever want to hurt you again."

The boys started pointing as the wagon pulled toward the cabins. Thom and Sarah were coming out the front door, smiling and waving.

"Home," Caroline sighed. "Home is where the heart is. My heart is here. Here in the mountains with the people who love me dearly. Here with the people that I love with all my heart."

Thank you, Lord. You brought spring into the valley and with spring came love.

Made in the USA
Coppell, TX
21 September 2023

21855352R00166